"Oh, Tru, I cannot help myself," Sasha sighed

Passion—recklessly ignited—was putting her in serious jeopardy yet even as she fought against that knowledge, she moved closer to Tru. "This is definitely not smart...."

"No, I suppose not." Tru attempted to sound resolute. He tried even harder to keep his hands off her alluring body. He struck out on both counts.

"If we were smart, Tru, would we be here together like this...?" An aching need enveloped her. Her hands, almost as if they weren't her own, crept up Tru's chest, across his shoulders, around his neck.

"This is...risky, Sasha."

"But we are attracted to risk, yes?" Sasha looked intently at Tru's face for confirmation.

Tru pulled her close, all remnant of caution dissolving, the desire he'd held in check evaporating in one breath. "Yes. Oh, yes, yes. Sasha, yes..."

Dear Reader,

Laughter and romance is a combination that has always hit the spot for me. Ever since I was a kid, I've had a love affair going with the marvellous screwball romantic films of the thirties and forties. The greatest fun and challenge for me has been to capture the humor of those movies and transplant them into contemporary romance novels. In the ten Temptation stories I've written to date, I've had a chance to let my madcap imagination run wild, combining lighthearted romance with some good old-fashioned slapstick.

The Fortune Boys series, in particular, is my loving tribute to all those bygone romantic comedies I adore. In these four books, I've taken each of four brothers in turn, all dyed-in-the-wool bachelors dripping with money, celebrity and success, and teamed them with four classy women with spirit, spunk and passion to spare. What happens after that is strictly chemistry, but I'll leave you to discover the outcome.

I hope you enjoy #412 *Adam & Eve*, #416 *For the Love of Pete*, #420 *True Love* and #424 *Taylor Made* (December 1992).

Sincerely,

Elise Title

P.S. I'd love to hear from my readers.

TRUE LOVE

ELISE TITLE

Harlequin Books

TORONTO • NEW YORK • LONDON
AMSTERDAM • PARIS • SYDNEY • HAMBURG
STOCKHOLM • ATHENS • TOKYO • MILAN
MADRID • WARSAW • BUDAPEST • AUCKLAND

Published November 1992

ISBN 0-373-25520-9

TRUE LOVE

Prologue

I REALLY DON'T KNOW WHY Doris is making such a fuss about this interview. Doris is my secretary—that little gray-haired woman who greeted you in my outer office. Been with the law firm since— Well, I shouldn't give the exact number of years. Doris is somewhat sensitive about her age and I wouldn't hear the end of it if the figure was to get printed in the paper—I mean, in the *Denver Star* magazine. It's Doris's favorite magazine. She probably told you that when you came in. She's very proud to say she's had a subscription since the magazine first came out in the sixties. Or was it the fifties?

Anyway, as I told your superior on the phone, I rarely give interviews, especially when it involves discussing clients. I hold to strict ethics when it comes to matters of confidentiality between attorney and client. But then, your superior assured me he had already received permission from the Fortunes for me to give an interview— I hope he wasn't offended that I checked on that myself. I suppose I'll be doing the family a service to set the record straight—considering there've been so many ridiculous stories about them in those scurrilous tabloids. So much has been written about the Fortune boys—much of it farfetched and unfounded—since word got out over a year ago of the tontine their father put in his will.

So, let me set the record straight. Alexander Fortune did not, as some articles have suggested, breathe a word of his plan to me—or to anyone else for that matter. No. Alexander was a man who kept his own counsel, although certainly if he was to have confided in anyone, I'd like to believe it would have been me. I wasn't only Alexander's lawyer for well on twenty years, but also his dear friend. He knew he could always rely on Nolan Fielding in a pinch. Not that I'm tooting my own horn, mind you. Oh, I can just hear Doris razzing me if that quote gets in your article. Let's say that was off the record.

Anyway, as for the tontine, I assure you he never told a soul. Especially not his mother, Jessica, or any of his four sons. You may wonder how I can be so sure. Well, young man, I witnessed their shock and outrage when I read the tontine to them.

As for the details of the tontine, I must say that's been done to death in the press. But just so that you can have my perspective, I shall give you a brief overview. You should understand that Alexander Fortune never did have much luck with women. Or wives, I should say. He had four wives, to be precise, and as he often confided to me, the only blessing he received from any of them was the son they each bore him. Alexander adored his four boys. And he was fortunate—pardon the pun—to be the parent to raise them, his four ex-wives all agreeing—and justifiably so if I may say—that the boys would be better off being looked after by their father. And, in my humble opinion, although I am a bachelor and know little about raising children, I will say for the record that I personally think Alexander did a fine job. With his mother Jessica's help, I must add.

Jessica has been, and remains to this day, a most formidable and persuasive presence in the boys' lives. Not that they don't adore her—which I assure you they all do. She had a direct hand in the marriages of both Adam and Peter. I dare say that if it weren't for her, neither of her grandsons would ever have tied the knot. But I'm getting ahead of myself—as Doris would be quick to point out.

Let's get back to the tontine business. There was the requisite reading of the will shortly after the funeral. However, Alexander had added a codicil to the will, which he stipulated wasn't to be read to the family until six months after his passing—to give the family proper mourning time. I imagine he knew the codicil would cause quite a stir; which, of course, it did. As for the will itself, there were no surprises there. Alexander left his mother a generous lifetime annuity, which, I might add— again off the record—leaves her an easy mark for unscrupulous fortune hunters. I have nothing more to say on that matter except to add that Doris has, on several occasions lately, voiced the same opinion. We were both rather dismayed to see Jessica—of course this is off the record—make rather a fool of herself with a particular gentleman at her grandson Peter's wedding last month. Mind you, off the record or not, I'm not a gossip and I shall name no names. Besides, I haven't been in the legal profession for over forty years not to realize that off-the-record information occasionally sneaks onto the record. Not that I'm doubting your ethics . . .

Where was I before I . . . veered off? Oh, yes. I was summing up Alexander's will. Jessica also was left the lavish family compound here in Denver. As for Alexander's four sons—Adam, Peter, Truman, and Taylor— they received the rest of the vast estate and Fortune Enterprises, now the fastest-growing chain of upscale department stores in the northwestern United States. Their fifteenth store opened this past month in Chicago. Peter's wedding celebration was held there in the haberdashery department the evening before the grand opening. My first wedding in a department store. And Doris's. Oh, she snickered a bit about the setting, saying a church wedding would have been more romantic, but I thought it was especially fitting, since you could say Peter and his bride, Elizabeth, met over the founding of that particular store. You see, Peter went out to Chicago to close the deal with Oppenheimer of Oppenheimer Lingerie and there was some crazy mix-up about his homburg—that is, Peter's homburg. I must confess I never did quite get all the details of the homburg incident straight. Poor Peter was cast out of his taxi in the middle of a storm—I believe the taxi driver might have been involved with drugs. But again, don't quote me on that or I'll likely end up with a lawsuit on my hands.

The long and the short of it is, Peter was struck by lightning and that's how he met Elizabeth, who was his doctor. From what little I heard, his condition caused some rather... bizarre behavioral changes. Oh, not bizarre in a *bizarre* way. Just bizarre for Peter. You see, the boy—there I go calling them boys again and I did promise Doris just before your arrival that I wouldn't do that. The Fortune boys are all in their thirties and Doris is quite right: They are men. Although some of the things Peter did out in Chicago after his unfortunate—again, pardon the pun—encounter with that lightning bolt, were rather boyish. I'm sure you saw that article that made the front pages of every newspaper in the country a few months back, didn't you? Peter Fortune crowned hero of the hour at a romance writers' convention. And there was that ridiculous photo of him in a crown and robe embracing Elizabeth like . . . well, like a romance hero.

I admit I didn't take it seriously. But Doris, if you interview her afterward, will point out to you that she predicted then and there that Peter would marry Elizabeth. Do you wonder that I pooh-poohed the notion? Peter give up everything for love? Never. Of course, his older brother, Adam, did just that only a year before him. Adam and Eve. Yes, that was a love story, all right. Then again, Adam was a born romantic. And with Jessica's devious plotting . . . Oh, yes, Jessica most definitely believes her grandsons should wed, have children, and live happily if poorly ever after. Jessica's own marriage was quite successful and she's a firm believer in the power and glory of love. Especially lately. But that's another story.

Anyway, once Jessica began scheming to get Adam wed, there was no question he'd be a goner. That whole amnesia act that she roped Eve into going along with, and which, I might add, Eve performed quite brilliantly . . . Well, I won't go into it again. There've been dozens of articles on that romance. I even heard some romance writer wrote a book about it. And rumor has it, there's going to be a sequel all about Peter and Elizabeth. I suppose this love-or-money theme is a powerful one.

Ah, but I haven't summed up the tontine for you yet. And so my references to Adam being a goner and Peter giving up everything for love won't make much sense to those new readers of yours unless they know about the tontine. Stated simply, Alexander devised a plan—a variation of a traditional tontine—which he believed would ensure that his sons wouldn't make the same mistake he'd made when it came to women. By mistake, I mean quite simply—marrying them. As I'm sure you al-

ready know, Alexander's tontine required that any son
who chose to marry would be required to forfeit all his
vast holdings to his single brothers. In a word—a few
words—it was to be an either-or choice. Love or money.
Ah, "money" is putting it lightly. I am not giving anything away in saying we are talking here about enor-
mous sums of money. And power, prestige, entry to the
finest circles— Well, you're a reporter. I'm sure you get
the picture. Mind you, all four sons, while being very
different personalities, have thoroughly enjoyed their
position and their wealth. For Adam, it meant—until his
marriage—being the playboy of Denver. For Peter, it
meant—until his marriage—being the president and
driving force of the Fortune Enterprises. Now there only
remains Truman and Taylor. Two down and two to go.
Doris's words, not mine. Grant you, after that tontine
business, I wouldn't have believed that I would have at-
tended even *one* Fortune wedding, never mind *two*.

I suppose you'd be justified in saying Alexander's tontine hasn't worked all that well, after all. But as for Truman and Taylor following in their brothers' footsteps,
here you can quote me as saying, I strongly doubt— No,
you can say, I firmly believe that neither Truman nor
Taylor will marry, period. I cannot imagine that even a
scheme devised by Jessica could work on those two dyed-
in-the-wool bachelors.

Take Truman. First of all, Tru, as he's called by his
friends, has always been the Fortune rebel of the clan. I'm
fond of Tru, as I am of all the boys. Still, there's no de-
nying Tru is brash, opinionated and outspoken, and he
has very little patience—especially when it comes to the
opposite sex, most of whom he's quick to deem frivolous and greedy. Tru's relationships with women have
invariably been brief. Not only has he never come close

to considering marriage, I seriously doubt any woman would have him. He's just too impulsive and...reckless. Even now, having inherited the presidency of Fortune's as the next heir in line, he still drives to work on his ghastly Harley motorcycle, dressed from head to toe in black leather, mind you. Doris, who's far and away more romantic than she lets on to most people, insists Tru's the spitting image of James Dean. She seems to think his mode of transportation—not to mention his hoodlum attire—is . . . sexy. Oh, dear. I shouldn't have said that. She'll deny using the word if you ask her, and then she won't let me hear the end of it. Let's forget I ever brought up James Dean.

Besides, Tru does change into something a bit more conservative, once he's at his office—suede sport coats and such. Still, quite a contrast to his brother Peter, who only wore his hallmark pin-striped suits when he was president of Fortune's. Although I hear that Peter has abandoned his conservative attire now. They always say marriage changes a man. Which, I might add, has gone a long way toward reinforcing my own state of bachelorhood.

Anyway, Tru has been itching to get control of Fortune's for years now. Thinks the company is behind the times and always felt Peter was far too conservative in his business management. Heaven only knows what Tru will do, now that he's in command.

Of course, Taylor has a say in what Tru does with Fortune's. Now that Adam and Peter have turned their shares over to their brothers, Tru and Taylor have a fifty-fifty split. But, to be truthful, Taylor doesn't really say all that much. He doesn't have a head for business. He's rather shy and reclusive. Not in an odd way, mind you. Taylor's an inventor. Why, at this very moment, he's working on an actual robot. It's his most ambitious undertaking to date. Mind you, his prior inventions haven't always been ... all he'd hoped, and there are those who think Taylor's creative spirit and ingenuous enthusiasm are greater than his actual creations. I will admit some of Taylor's inventions have backfired. And others have been somewhat too ... specialized. Like his electric can opener designed strictly for sardine cans. Then again, if you've ever tried opening a sardine can with one of those key contraptions ... Taylor was kind enough to give me the prototype, but unfortunately, I for one don't really care for sardines.

Anyway, that's neither here nor there. The point I'm trying to make, pure and simple, is that neither Tru nor Taylor are the marrying kind. Taylor rarely comes out of his laboratory for air, much less any serious dating. And you can be assured that Tru has his guard up solidly against any of his grandmother's matchmaking schemes. As he's told her right to her face, she won't be able to play Cupid with him, so she shouldn't ever bother trying. Even given Jessica's success with her other two grandsons, I quite agree.

On this—as on most things—Doris and I don't see exactly eye to eye. Doris believes, in the end, love always wins out. But then, as I said before, Doris is far too much of a romantic. You can quote me as saying, the last two Fortune boys will definitely remain single.

I daresay Doris will be only too happy to give you permission to quote her saying just the opposite. I do hope she isn't proved right. She'll never let me hear the end of that one ...

1

SASHA MALZEVA CHEESEMAN remained sitting rigidly in her seat on the plane as the other passengers swarmed into the aisles. She was in no hurry. In truth, she was somewhat nervous. All right, quite nervous. She was determined to appear composed and undaunted by her decidedly daunting situation when she met her hostess, Mrs. Jessica Fortune, for the first time.

The plane was almost empty and Sasha saw the stewardess approaching, no doubt to ask her if there was any problem. She quickly rose to avoid a discussion, tightly gripping her heavy but compact worn leather satchel, and stepped into the aisle with a formal nod in the stewardess's direction.

As she walked slowly down the long passageway that linked the plane and the terminal, Sasha again went over in her mind just how she would describe to her grandmother's schoolgirl friend the humiliating and distressing situation that brought her here. Oh, she'd written a letter giving the briefest of explanations for her requested visit, but the details... She fervently hoped that Mrs. Fortune would not immediately bombard her with questions. Sasha could feel her cheeks warm as she thought of some of those questions as well as some of her answers, and she had to stop to compose herself. She certainly didn't want to impress Jessica Fortune as being a foolish, flighty, impetuous young Russian woman when she was, in truth, none of those things—except for one brief and all-too-disastrous moment . . . or two.

MADISON, WHO'D BEEN Jessica Fortune's chauffeur for over thirty years, stood just outside the arrivals gate, blowing his nose discreetly into his linen handkerchief. He'd had the sniffles for over a week now, although it was nothing serious, just annoying. When the first passengers began to exit through the swing doors, he hastily stowed his handkerchief in his back trouser pocket and carefully smoothed down his navy uniform. Madison, whose father and grandfather had also been chauffeurs, took great pride in following in their footsteps and felt an admitted degree of smugness about how well he carried on the family tradition.

After lifting a small black-lettered sign over his head that read, Sasha Malzeva Cheeseman, Madison began examining each young female face in the crowd. He knew the young woman he was to meet was in her mid-twenties, and although Mrs. Fortune had never seen her or even a photo of her, she had shown him an old photograph of the young woman's grandmother at about the same age. If Sasha Malzeva Cheeseman in any way resembled her grandmother, then she was going to be a real knockout. Not that Madison had said as much to his employer when he inspected the photo; just some appropriate pleasantry about the young woman's grandmother being a fine-looking woman. Of course, Jessica Fortune had given him one of her looks—after thirty years, he couldn't get much past her. Still, what was said between them and what was privately thought were two different things.

A shapely young woman with ash-blond hair and a vivacious smile was just coming through the swing doors. Madison felt certain this was his charge and angled the sign toward her, smiling discreetly.

As it turned out, he was mistaken about the pretty blonde. She breezed right past him into the waiting arms of a handsome, well-dressed young man standing a few feet behind him. Madison continued surveying the other exiting passengers.

When it appeared the plane had emptied, Madison despaired that his charge had missed her flight. Just as he was about to leave to inquire into the matter, the doors swung open and a tall, slender young woman strode purposefully out. Madison, not one who was easily surprised, was admittedly taken aback by this severe, somber-looking woman. Her light blond hair was pulled back from her face into a schoolmarmish bun, and she was dressed in a drab, unflattering brown skirt and blouse with absolutely no adornment whatsoever. Madison was sure of one thing: She hadn't bought the outfit at Fortune's. More likely the Salvation Army. Could this really be the granddaughter of that winsome, vivacious young woman he'd seen in the old photograph? Apparently she was, for she was heading right toward him, her eyes on the sign that he had quickly resurrected.

Madison politely reached out for the young woman's suitcase only to find her grabbing his hand in a hearty handshake.

"I am most happy to meet you. You are the husband of Mrs. Jessica Fortune?" Sasha inquired in a low, smoky, heavily accented voice.

Madison flushed. "Hus-band? Oh, no. I am in Mrs. Fortune's service."

Sasha gave him a scrutinizing look that Madison found uncomfortably intimidating.

"I'm Madison, Mrs. Fortune's chauffeur," he added, thinking she might not understand.

Sash continued her study. "You are too old to be in service. Is there no retirement for one so aged?"

"Oh, I—uh—assure you, I'm quite—fit," the chauffeur stammered.

Sasha raised a darker blond eyebrow as she shook her head and gave him a pitying look.

Afraid that she would grab his hand again, Madison politely asked if he might take her bag.

Again she raised a brow. "Where would you take it?" she asked somberly.

"I meant, may I carry it for you?"

"Certainly not," she declared firmly. "You should be resting in the sun, enjoying your last years in peace and tranquility, little father, not having to carry about a healthy young person's luggage. There is no purpose to such a job that I can see."

"Well . . . it isn't my only job. I also drive the Fortune family—"

"They do not know how to drive?" Sasha demanded.

"Well, no. I mean . . . yes. But really, madam . . ."

Patting his shoulder, she said, "You must call me comrade. We are both workers." She gave him a firm look. "You must gather together with your aged brothers, little father, and demand your just rights."

"Uh . . . yes, madam—I mean—comrade." He felt a sneeze coming on and quickly turned from her, extracting his handkerchief just in the nick of time, after which he murmured an apology.

Sasha gave him a sympathetic look. "You are sick, yes?"

"Oh, just a summer cold," he assured her. "If you have your baggage tickets I can claim the rest of your luggage and we can be on our way."

"We are ready now. I have no other luggage."

As Madison led the way to the exit, he could hear her muttering, "Old and sick and still in servitude . . ."

Unfortunately, a few minutes later, Madison had a sneezing attack just as he was opening the rear door of the limo for his passenger.

Before he knew what was happening, she was practically pushing him into the back seat, demanding the keys to the car. "You are in no condition to drive. It is ridiculous when I am a perfectly capable driver. Why should you, a poor, old, infirm man, have to?"

"You have the wrong impression, madam," Madison protested, trying to step out of the back of the car, only to have Sasha block his exit.

"Comrade," she reminded him, bending down and pulling off his shoes before he realized what he was up to. "Do not be nervous, little father. I am a very good driver. In Russia I have driven trucks, jeeps, even once a bus." She held out her hand for the key, her expression broaching no further argument.

"It's most—irregular, madam—comrade," Madison muttered. However, seeing the resolute expression on her face, he felt he had no other recourse but to meekly hand over the keys. All he could do was pray that no one in the family found out.

TRUMAN FORTUNE gunned his Harley as the light turned green and weaved in and out of the late-afternoon traffic. He was turning onto Laurel Street when he was startled to spot his grandmother's limo zipping along up ahead of him. Tru had never known Madison to even come close to the speed limit before. Deciding to rib him a bit for having his pedal to the metal, Tru checked to make sure there was no oncoming traffic, then sped ahead to catch up.

Tru pulled close to the driver's side, surprised to see the window open. When a dour-looking female driver gave him a sharp look and called him a crazy bourgeois idiot in a thick foreign accent, he assumed he'd mistaken the car—until he spotted the abashed and all-too-familiar Madison trying to slink down as low as possible in the rear seat.

Tru was so astonished, he almost lost control of his motorcycle. A van was coming toward him and Tru nearly crashed into the limo as he cut back into the proper lane just in the nick of time.

SASHA GLARED AT THE brash biker as he alighted from his motorcycle. *What audacity, to pursue her right up to the Fortune house!*

"You are a very reckless driver," Sasha declared sharply. "You might have gotten me and my sick old friend killed by your idiotic daredevil stunt. In Russia you would be arrested for such driving. But I suppose you are one of those . . . Hell's Angels I have read about. Like Marlon Brando. I have seen American films." She focused on his open black leather motorcycle jacket. "Oh, yes, I know how you hooligans race about on your motorcycles, caring nothing for society's rules, causing havoc, terrifying innocent people. . . ."

Tru broke into laughter. "A Hell's Angel? Oh, that's priceless!"

"Yes, you laugh. But I pity you. You are a very sad product of the decadence and corruption that is systemic in your society. But, remember, it is never too late to be rehabilitated. You are a young, healthy, strong man. Do you not want to contribute anything beneficial to society, comrade? Do you want to be always a useless, unproductive citizen?"

Tru couldn't believe the woman was serious, but she didn't so much as crack a smile as she issued her doctrinaire challenge. He gave her a teasing look. "I'm a reckless driver? Do you know, comrade, that you were going forty in a thirty-mile zone? In this country, speeding is quite a serious offense. If a cop had come along, he'd have hauled you in and you could have spent thirty days in the slammer, with nothing to eat but that real cheap kind of white bread and water."

Sasha gave him a cautious look. "I do not believe this is true that I was speeding. I saw no sign."

"That's because you roared right by it, comrade. And, anyway, for a while there, I thought you were kidnapping Madison." At that precise moment, Madison opened the back door and sheepishly exited.

Shoes in hand, Madison gave Tru a helpless look. "She—uh—insisted on driving, sir. She was . . . most persuasive."

Tru didn't doubt it. As he looked back at the young woman, he saw that she was now digging out a bottle of Russian vodka from her satchel. He then watched in stunned silence as she foisted the bottle on Madison, who was still struggling into his shoes.

"Here, little father. You will drink this and you will feel better. Now you must rest. Surely, even when you are not yet allowed retirement, you are permitted time to recover from illness." Before Madison could assure her that he wasn't really ill and that his employer was more than generous when it came to sick leave, the front door opened and Jessica Fortune stepped outside.

Madison quickly stuck the bottle of vodka behind his back as his employer approached the group.

"Sasha, welcome," Jessica said warmly, embracing Sasha who stiffened in response. "I see you've already met Tru."

Sasha once again eyed the wild motorcycle driver. "Tru?"

Jessica bit back a laugh as her grandson looked over at her. "No, we haven't exactly met," Tru replied, a faint, mocking smile flashing across his face.

IT WAS NEARLY SEVEN that evening when Tru came skidding to a stop on his Harley in front of his grandmother's house. He'd promised her the day before that he'd come over for dinner tonight. He'd thought it an innocent invitation at the time, but now that he'd inadvertently had a run-in with his grandmother's new houseguest, he knew differently. The dinner was a setup—an arranged meeting with the dour Russian "comrade." Surely his grandmother couldn't believe there were any matchmaking possibilities here. Okay, he'd done more than his share of ranting and raving about the frivolous, scatterbrained young women he usually spent time with. And granted, this Russian import appeared anything but. Still, she wasn't exactly winning in his estimation—in either appearance or personality.

"Tru? Is that you?" his grandmother called out from the sun porch. "We're out here."

Reluctantly, Tru headed in that direction.

There she was, sitting rigidly and solemnly on one side of a large wicker chaise, her knees pressed together, her hands folded primly on her lap, her back ramrod straight. She was no longer wearing that ghastly brown skirt-and-blouse set, but her new outfit—a somber gray cotton dress and matching jacket—was not what he would call a vast improvement.

Jessica poured her grandson a glass of wine and motioned him to sit on the chaise beside Sasha. On the wicker table in front of them was an open photograph album.

"I was just showing Sasha these old photos of me and her grandmother when we were schoolmates in Switzerland," Jessica said, pulling up her chair beside Tru. She lifted the open album, angling it toward her grandson. "Most of these were taken during our senior picnic. We went to this lovely spot on Lake Lucerne. Oh, I remember it like it was yesterday," she murmured, pointing to a photo of a group of girls leaning against the rail of a tour boat on the lake. "There we are, all twenty of us, along the rail. Well, there were twenty-one of us, actually, but Gail Endicott was terrified of water so she refused to go on the boat. She took the picture from the shore."

Tru lifted the album to examine the picture more closely. "Which one's you? Oh, wait. There you are," Tru said, pointing to a pretty fair-haired girl who was waving gaily toward shore.

"Very good, Tru," Jessica replied with a smile.

Tru patted her hand affectionately. "You haven't changed one iota. You're still the prettiest girl around."

"You're not very good at flattery, Truman. It's not your style."

Tru could feel Sasha's eyes on him and guessed that she was thinking the same thing. Not that he cared what she was thinking, he told himself.

"Now, see if you can place Leila," Jessica prodded.

"Who?" Tru asked.

"Sasha's grandmother. See if you can spot the resemblance between the two."

Tru reluctantly studied the photo again. Twenty bright, youthful, feminine faces. Some were pretty, others plain, but none of those faces in any way resembled the solemn, humorless, stiff Sasha. But then he found his finger stopping at one face. The girl wasn't so much beautiful as vital. There was an exuberance about her, a spiritedness. Really the complete opposite of the dour Sasha, but there was something in the eyes....

Jessica smiled as she saw her grandson's gaze move from the photo to Sasha, whose response was to stiffen even more.

"We are really nothing alike," Sasha muttered.

Jessica gazed reminiscently at the photo. "Your grandmother was my very closest school friend. Oh, she was such a flamboyant, bohemian girl. Shortly before we graduated from boarding school in Switzerland she declared herself a communist and right after graduation defected to Russia," she explained to Tru.

Sasha sighed. "She was a wonderful woman and a fine comrade who never lacked for political reliability and always followed strict party line." Sasha smiled, remembering that for all that, throughout her life her grandmother remained a bit wild, a bit flamboyant, and yes, a bit of a romantic. Sasha feared she was more like her grandmother than she would ever want to admit.

Jessica picked up the hint of distress in Sasha's expression and tactfully changed the subject. Closing the album and depositing it back on the coffee table, she turned to Tru. "Sasha was just going to explain the dilemma she briefly wrote me about in her letter."

Sasha could not quite conceal her alarm. "Oh, I am sure your grandson would not be...interested. Perhaps, later—"

"Nonsense, Sasha. You said in your letter that you had a most troubling and perplexing problem, and Tru is extremely bright, knowledgeable and excellent at problem solving."

Tru gave his grandmother a dark look. "Your usual line is to say I get into more problems than I get out of, Gran. Anyway, I don't want to butt into someone else's business. And maybe Sasha is right. She might feel more comfortable—" He started to rise, eager to be off before his grandmother roped him into anything.

Sasha refused to allow this indifferent man to think that he could make her uncomfortable even if she was feeling...uncomfortable. "Perhaps it is conceivable you will have a worthwhile suggestion."

It was partly the challenge he felt in Sasha's dubiously voiced remark that brought him back to his seat, and partly the forceful tug on his sleeve by his grandmother.

When he looked at Sasha again, Tru was disconcerted to note that her eyes, which were an unusual shade of blue, almost aquamarine, were very much like her grandmother's eyes. But the resemblance ended there, Tru realized, noting the grim line of Sasha's mouth, which was in sharp contrast to that of the smiling, vivacious Leila. He wondered if the dour comrade ever smiled. And he couldn't for the life of him imagine her ever enjoying a good old belly laugh.

"So, what is this problem that I might conceivably be able to help you with?" he asked dryly.

Sasha hesitated. "I have come here to find my...husband."

"Husband? You're...married?" Well, the woman knew how to throw a curve.

Jessica withdrew a photograph from her skirt pocket. She passed it to Tru. He took hold of it gingerly, then proceeded to stare at it for a long time.

"It's a wedding photo," he muttered. To be more precise, it was a photo of Sasha looking a good deal more attractive—under other circumstances Tru might even have chosen the word *luminescent*—in a flowing white satin wedding gown. Beside her was a dapper, handsome groom outfitted in a well-cut tuxedo. The pair stood on the steps of an official-looking building.

"The man is Drew Cheeseman. He vanished on their wedding night," Jessica said, giving Sasha a sympathetic smile.

Tru regarded the photo more intently, then looked over at Sasha, finding it hard to reconcile this grim woman beside him with the lovely-looking bride in the picture. For a moment he lost his train of thought. "Vanished?" he muttered, after a long pause.

"Yes. Vanished," Sasha replied, pursing her lips, determined to not reveal how humiliated she felt about Drew's disappearance.

"And you think he's here? In the States?" Despite his vow not to get involved, Tru was so overcome by curiosity, the question just slipped out.

Sasha knew that she had to get the whole story out as quickly and mundanely as possible or her discomfort would get the better of her. Forcing herself to level her gaze on Tru, she began her account as she might have begun a journal report. "Drew Cheeseman is an American businessman. We met in Moscow. At a joint convention of Russian-American farm-machinery manufacturers. We—"

"Farm-machinery manufacturers?" Tru interrupted. "Is that what you do? Sell farm machinery?" It figured, he thought.

Sasha gave him an arch look. "No. I am a journalist. I was assigned to cover this convention for my paper. Agricultural affairs are my specialty."

"Yes, well, go on, my dear," Jessica urged. "You and Drew met at this convention and . . . ?"

Sasha's fingers fluttered nervously for a moment, but she quickly steadied them. She looked at Tru briefly and then chose, instead, to focus on Jessica. "We found we had much in common. We enjoyed each other's company. . . very much." Even though she wasn't looking at Tru, she could sense his wry smile. Irritated, she turned abruptly to him, offering an unmistakable challenge. "It has not happened to you?" she demanded formidably.

Tru hadn't expected a direct attack and was thrown off guard. "Yes— I mean, no— That is, I've never enjoyed someone's company enough to marry them. How long did you know this character, anyway, before the two of you got hitched?"

Sasha hesitated before answering because her reply sorely embarrassed her. Assuming she hadn't understood his slang, Tru explained. "Got hitched. Tied the knot. Got married."

Sasha managed a faint smile. Tru couldn't help noticing that the smile, however brief and elusive, improved her appearance considerably. "I am most obliged to you, Tru, for your lesson in idiomatic English."

Tru eyed her knowingly. "You're hedging, Comrade Cheeseman. Something tells me this worldly, handsome American breezed into your politically reliable, socially conscious life and swept you right off your comradely feet. And my guess is," he gibed, "that was no mean feat."

"Tru!" Jessica scolded sharply.

But Tru merely shrugged. "I'm only saying that Sasha seems the sort of woman who generally has her feet planted solidly on the ground. Or should I say, on the rich, fertilized soil of her nation?"

Sasha recognized perfectly well that he was being deliberately rude—no doubt to make her lose her composure. While she did find his flippant manner—not to mention his good looks—disturbing, she was certainly not about to give him the satisfaction of showing that he was unnerving her. Nor did she wish to acknowledge that he was correct. She wasn't the least bit proud of her reckless, irresponsible behavior with Drew. How could she, such a serious-minded journalist dedicated to the agrarian development of her country, have let herself fall prey to such passion—such folly? Well all she could do now was vow that nothing like that would ever happen to her again.

She gave Tru a patronizing look. "Drew and I found ourselves to be very compatible even though we did not know each other for an exceedingly long time. He asked me to marry him, agreeing to stay as much as possible in Moscow with me, and I accepted in good faith that we would have a . . . good marriage."

"But not a very long one," Tru muttered acerbically. And then, realizing he had gone a step too far, he muttered a hasty apology.

"Then tell me, Tru. Do most marriages in America last a long time? Is it not true that most American marriages fail dismally?"

"You bet. That's why those of us who have any common sense know better than to marry," Tru said glibly.

"Oh. So you are saying I do not have common sense?" Sasha challenged.

"I'm saying—"

"You were saying that you were sorry for your rude remark, Truman," Jessica interjected, afraid they might come to blows if she didn't referee.

Jessica turned to Sasha with a sympathetic look. "It must have been awful for you, Sasha, dear. And on your wedding night, no less. But you wrote in your letter that he did give you an explanation."

"It must have been a doozie," Tru said snidely.

Jessica gave him a warning look. Sasha raised a brow, knowing his remark was cutting, even though she didn't know the meaning of the word *doozie*.

Still, she found this part easier to discuss. It was the foolish, headstrong, irresponsible whirlwind courtship that she didn't want to dwell on, especially in Tru's presence. She saw Jessica's encouraging smile and, looking directly at her, she began her story.

"On our wedding night, we stayed in one of the fine hotels in Moscow. Shortly after we arrived, even before our suitcases were brought up, Drew excused himself to go down to the lobby to make a business call."

"Don't fine Moscow hotels have room phones?" Tru asked sarcastically.

"Really, Tru," Jessica snapped.

Sasha gave him an icy stare. "It was a private call."

"Sounds a bit cloak-and-dagger to me," Tru commented lightly. But then he saw Sasha's whole demeanor change. There was even a sharp intake of breath.

Magnetized by her reaction, Tru scrutinized her more closely, as if trying to penetrate a disguise. "Is that it? Did it turn out that this guy was a spy?"

"Oh, dear," Jessica murmured with a blend of dismay and excitement.

Sasha pressed one of her hands over the other, trying to stem the trembling. And to hide it from Tru's eyes. "Perhaps . . . something . . . worse."

"Worse?" Tru and Jessica exclaimed in unison.

"You must allow me to explain the proper sequence of events," Sasha said forcefully.

Her tone was so commanding, Tru, as well as Jessica, found himself nodding contritely.

"I did not think anything untoward of Drew's request to make a private business call. But he did not return. Nearly an hour goes by. And then there is a knock on my door. A boy gives me a note from Drew." Sasha omitted saying how she had foolishly rushed to open the door and nearly fell into the arms, not of her new husband but of the timid messenger boy, who nervously extended the note to her, then fled as if she'd meant to seduce him.

"So," Tru said impatiently, "what did the note say?"

"Don't rush her, Tru. I'm sure this is very difficult for Sasha," Jessica admonished.

"The note says that there is a serious emergency and he must return to Chicago immediately."

Jessica glanced at Tru who, she was pleased to see, was listening with rapt attention. She'd guessed it wouldn't be all that difficult to engage him in Sasha's plight. She did wish, though, that the girl were a bit less rigid and dogmatic. But she imagined Tru would loosen her up in time.

"That's it?" Tru prompted.

"No," Sasha replied. "He asked that I pick up his luggage back at the room he was staying in before our wedding and requested that I fly to Chicago in three days to meet him."

"So you went to Chicago?" Tru asked, totally curious now.

"No," Sasha said. "I gave it very careful consideration, but as I told Drew from the start, I do not wish to leave Moscow. I have a very good job and I am committed to helping my country out of its recent economic problems. So I telephoned Drew in Chicago to tell him that he must settle his emergency and then return to Moscow as he agreed."

"And he refused?" Tru asked.

"He didn't refuse. I never spoke to him. I called his company and they told me they do not have any person by the name of Drew Cheeseman working there. They said," she added in a lower voice, "they never heard of Drew Cheeseman and that no representative from their company was sent to the convention in Moscow." She paused, remembering the shock of it, the humiliation of having been deceived. And then, later, to learn that that wasn't the worst of it.

"And there were no listings for him in the Chicago phone book?"

This time Jessica answered Tru's question. "No. I checked soon after I received Sasha's letter."

"It could be an unlisted number," Tru pointed out.

"Unlisted?" Sasha looked baffled.

"My friend from Chicago, Ben Engel, knows someone on the Chicago police force and he had him do some further checking," Jessica explained. "There is no record of a Drew Cheeseman living or working in Chicago or the surrounding area. For whatever reason, this man obviously handed poor Sasha a pack of lies. He married her and deserted her, all within twenty-four hours. It's quite despicable."

But Tru sensed there was still more to the story. "How about cutting to the chase, Sasha."

She gave him a perplexed look.

"You found something out about this character, even if you don't know where he is. Right?"

"Tru," Jessica warned, "may I remind you this man you are calling a 'character' happens to be Sasha's husband—for better or worse."

"It sounds like for worse," Tru said dryly.

Jessica was about to scold him again, when Sasha interrupted. "Tru is correct, Mrs. Fortune." Sasha's staunch composure faltered for a moment.

Neither of the Fortunes spoke, both waiting with bated breath for the kicker.

Sasha then methodically described how she decided to retrieve her husband's belongings from his room and examine them more thoroughly back in her own quarters, a small apartment in Moscow that she shared with four other women—all journalists dedicated to the future economic, social and political betterment of their country.

"I found very little," she explained when she finally got to a discussion of Cheeseman's belongings. "Some expensive white shirts, good-quality one-hundred-percent cotton underwear, three silk ties, and even the socks were made of a fine silk-and-wool blend." She gave Tru's attire—jeans and a scruffy blue work shirt—a rueful look.

Tru grinned. "Okay, so hubby was a real snappy dresser. You know what we say in this country? You can't always tell a book by its cover. What else did you find?" he urged, certain she'd discovered more than a few items of fine apparel among his belongings. And he was right.

In her low, smoky voice, Sasha almost whispered, "An eighteenth-century Russian icon. Quite small. Quite valuable. In a secret compartment in his toiletries case."

Tru stared intently at Sasha. "You think he was trying to smuggle it out." But then, before Sasha could reply, he said, "No, wait. He was shrewder than that. He wanted you to smuggle the piece into the States. Sure. That was the deal."

"Why, that's terrible," Jessica exclaimed. "What if a customs agent had discovered it in her possession?"

"Yes," Sasha said solemnly. "What if, exactly."

"I guess he figured it was better than him getting nabbed," Tru mused. "And if she did get through; he'd claim his new bride and probably a cool million bucks or more." Tru didn't say it, but he also guessed that Sasha wouldn't stay a bride for long, once her mate got his hands on the goods.

"Well, this is a very serious matter best left to the authorities, Sasha," Jessica said firmly.

But Sasha shook her head. "No, I do not trust authorities. What if it is believed that I am my husband's partner in crime? Do you know what the punishment is for attempted smuggling of a rare icon that belongs to the state?" She leveled her gaze on Tru. "Much greater than thirty days in a slammer with bad bread and water."

"Maybe he wasn't smuggling it," Jessica offered. "Is it possible it might have been planted among his possessions by someone else? A smuggler who was using Drew as a front? I've read of that happening in spy novels. Or maybe he bought it in good faith from some con artist and had no idea just how valuable—"

"Then why hide it?" Tru pointed out.

"Well, he may have been trying to sneak it in without paying the duty. I imagine it would be quite high," Jessica countered.

"Whatever his explanation," Sasha cut in, "I must find Drew and insist he come back with me to Russia where he will return the icon to its rightful owner so that my reputation and good name will go untarnished."

Tru gave her a derisive look. "And then what? The two of you live happily ever after in comradely wedded bliss?"

JESSICA HAD BEEN CALLED away to the phone as they were about to go in for dinner. She insisted that Tru escort Sasha to the dining room and that they start without her.

They sat across from each other, both feeling awkward and uneasy now that they were alone. Sasha broke the silence after their dinners were brought out by Jessica's housekeeper.

"You think I am a foolish woman," Sasha said so forthrightly Tru actually blushed.

"No. No, that's not true, Sasha. You don't impress me as a foolish woman in the least. I suppose you were just blinded by... love. I've got a couple of brothers who'd sympathize with you wholeheartedly."

"I think you would not be so foolish as I... or your couple of brothers, yes?"

"No. I mean...yes. Wait... Let me try again," Tru said, catching her smiling and finding it irritating. "How long did you know this guy before you married him, anyway?"

Sasha knew it was a question he would persist in asking until she told him. Better to merely answer without any extraneous explanations. In any case, she had no explanation. What had happened still made no sense to her. "Two weeks," she stated while she proceeded to meticulously cut into her steak, avoiding what she felt certain would be Tru's mocking expression.

FOR A FEW MINUTES TRU incorporated the rhythmic thrashing sound into his dream, then he awoke with a start. The thrashing sound was still in his head. It took a moment for him to realize it was a real sound, actually coming from outside the house. He squinted in the direction of his clock. Five forty-five? Five forty-five on a Sunday morning? Irritably he got out of bed and shuffled sleepily over to his window, drew aside the curtain and looked out to see what could be making that dull, annoying noise.

He rubbed his eyes. There, with dawn just cresting over the mountains, was Sasha, pushing an ancient manual lawn mower up and down over a small meadow.

Tru threw on a pair of shorts and went to his front door. He stood there, in his open doorway, just watching her. Today, Sasha's attire was no more fashionable than it had been the day before. She wore a pair of loose-fitting blue shorts and a blue running jacket. But it wasn't the outfit that drew his attention. It was her shapely, muscular legs. Not the result of workouts in a fancy fitness center. No. Sasha had the kind of muscles that came from solid, hard work. He remained there, watching her steady pace as she pushed the mower through the overgrown grass. She was halfway through the meadow and yet she didn't seem the least bit tired.

It surprised him when she suddenly stopped and swung around in his direction. The rising sun must have been in her eyes, for she cupped them over her brows as she looked straight at him. She made no gesture of greeting, nor could Tru make out so much as a smile.

Feeling embarrassed, as if he'd been caught spying on her, he waved with an utterly false cheeriness and started toward her.

He could see her tensing as he approached. She pushed a damp curl from her eyes. He'd thought by the way she'd worn her hair pulled back severely the day before that it must be straight. Now, seeing the few strands of hair curling around her face, he realized he'd been wrong.

"We have an electric mower. One of those huge contraptions you just have to sit on and ride. If that's your thing," Tru said, eyeing the ancient mower with its rusty blades, "I don't think that baby's been used in fifty years."

"It is a pity to let a good machine lie idle and in such poor repair."

"Is it jet lag or do all Russians get up before the crack of dawn?" Tru asked quickly, hoping to cut Sasha off at the pass.

"And Americans? Do you sleep all day and party all night?"

"Only when we can," he said with a wry smile. "Not when someone's pushing a creaky lawn mower up and down our meadow."

"I do not want to remain idle while I am here. This is good land. Good for planting. It is my way of repaying your kindly grandmother for her hospitality."

"My grandmother would be mortified if she thought you felt you needed to work to earn your keep."

"Your grandmother is most kind, but I hope I do not have to be here very long. She will have me meet with a private investigator tomorrow and hopefully, he will be of assistance to me."

Maybe it was the thought that she would be gone soon that made him impulsively invite her in for breakfast.

Sasha deliberated before she consented. He let her make up her mind on her own, offering only a shrug and a smile.

"HOW'S THE COFFEE?"

"It is good coffee," Sasha said. "Not strong like Russian coffee, but good." She set the cup down and looked at her omelet. "But this American cheese, I don't know."

He grinned. "An acquired taste."

She nodded, not cracking a smile. "You eat like this every Sunday?"

"Me, personally?"

"Americans?"

"Some Americans eat like this every day. But too many eggs and dairy products aren't supposed to be good for you. Cholesterol."

"In Russia, that is no problem. There is a great shortage of eggs and dairy products for most of my people."

"Well, while you're here you should eat as much of everything as you want."

"No. I have as much of everything as I want," she said in her typical sober fashion. She bit into her omelet, chewed, and then she shook her head. "No, not everything. I want to find Drew Cheeseman."

"If that's even his real name. It might not be so easy tracking him down, Sasha. And it could be dangerous."

Sasha gave him a defiant look. "You think I am afraid?"

Tru studied her thoughtfully. "No," he said finally, thinking he had never before met a woman who exuded such an air of self-confidence, containment and authority. Intriguing. Still, he couldn't imagine this formidable comrade being swept off her feet and losing her heart to a man she hardly knew. "He must have been quite a charmer, this Drew Cheeseman or whatever his name is."

"Yes," Sasha replied solemnly.

Tru took a swallow of coffee, observing her from over the rim of his cup.

"So, tell me, comrade," he said teasingly. "Are you pleased or disappointed that I'm not a wild Hell's Angel biker?"

Sasha once again didn't crack a smile. Indeed, with utmost seriousness, she answered, "I do not know. Perhaps I will not be here long enough to find out."

Their gazes locked and held. Tru felt an odd sensation, like the floor had suddenly tilted slightly. Everything was just a little off kilter. "Maybe," he said in a low voice, "that's just as well."

Sasha could feel her heartbeat pick up. A bad sign. "Yes," she replied gravely.

2

"I'M COUNTING ON YOUR support, Taylor," Tru said,
pacing up and down his younger brother's laboratory.
The lab occupied the entire basement of the carriage
house that Taylor had converted into his residence.

Taylor, surrounded by nuts, bolts, wires, and assorted electronic equipment, pushed his steel-rimmed
magnifying eyeglasses up on top of his head and squinted
at Tru. "I still don't see what you're worried about."

Tru gave his brother an astonished look. "You don't
see? You don't see what I'm worried about? Taylor, where
were you when Eve went waltzing down the aisle with
Adam? Or when Elizabeth and Peter went from a hot-air
balloon to the altar in one swift breeze?"

"But you don't even like this woman. You don't find
her particularly attractive or appealing. You said she's
stubborn, dogmatic, can't get a joke. . . ."

"I know, I know, but still . . ."

"Come on, Tru. You sound as if Granny's going to slip
you a magic love potion and suddenly you're going to
look at this Sasha and instead of seeing a plain, dour
comrade, you're going to see a gorgeous, vibrant
woman."

Tru didn't want to admit, even to himself, that there
were already moments . . .

Taylor began tinkering with his robot again, immediately losing himself in his work. Tru watched him for
a few moments, thinking that life was so easy and un-

complicated for Taylor. He sighed. "I left those papers for you to sign about the new promotional campaign. Did you get to them?"

Taylor gave him a distracted look. "Get what?"

"I need your okay on the new ad campaign. And while I think of it, you still haven't gone through the revisions on our overseas catalog. I know these minor details don't really interest you, Taylor—"

"I did go through the catalog. I thought it was fine. But then, it would probably be good to get a foreigner's opinion? Hey, wait—"

"Oh, no," Tru said, backing up toward the door. "Don't even suggest it, Taylor. I'm making a solemn vow right here and now to have absolutely nothing more to do with Comrade Sasha Cheeseman."

He might have kept that vow—at least for a few hours—if he hadn't literally stumbled over her twenty yards from the carriage house. It was Sasha's quick, strong grip on his arm that kept him from falling face-down in the newly tilled soil.

"What the... What are you up to now?" he demanded.

Sasha wasn't intimidated by his manner. "This is good, rich soil for vegetables. All this land, and I see you have no vegetable garden. Do you know how many people could be fed from your land?"

"Vegetables? Now you're planting vegetables?"

"Tomorrow. Today I prepare the soil."

"I thought my grandmother was taking you to see the shamus today."

"Shamus? Oh, yes. Like Humphrey Bogart. The private investigator."

"Don't you think all of this . . . farming . . . is interfering with your real purpose in being here? You do want to track down your husband, don't you?"

Sasha scrutinized him. "You like to argue, yes?"

"No," he snapped. "I'm not arguing. I don't argue. I'm merely pointing out . . . Reminding you . . ." His features darkened. "We don't need a vegetable garden, Sasha. There's a fine selection of every vegetable you can think of in a dozen supermarkets within a ten-mile radius of here."

"Why buy vegetables if you can grow your own vegetables? It is cheaper, better for the soil, better for you, good for your people. Do you think it is right to have so much and share so little, comrade?" She gave him a condescending look.

Tru could feel his blood begin to boil. "I'm not the one who likes to argue. It's you. You seem to take great pleasure in—in driving me crazy," he said, then stomped off.

"Tru!" she called out.

He considered not stopping, but even he could take rudeness only so far. So he stopped but didn't turn to face her. "Yes?"

"I do very much want to see this shamus your grandmother has so much confidence in. And more than anything I want to find Drew Cheeseman...or whatever his name is. But your grandmother was unable to do this today. She is with child."

Tru did turn around then, giving Sasha an incredulous stare. "With child? My grandmother is seventy-three years old, Sasha. You must have misunderstood. She's a little old to be pregnant, don't you think?"

"Pregnant?" Sasha pressed her lips together. Then she smiled. Not one of those brief flashes—a real smile. "Oh, Tru, you can be a very funny man."

"I'm funny? I'm not the one who said she's with child," he retorted, Sasha's vibrant smile drawing him closer like a magnet. In a moment he was standing beside her.

"I never said pregnant. I said with child. With a *neighbor's* child. What do you say—baby-sitting?" She was still smiling, with loose strands of blond hair that had escaped her barrette curling around her face.

Tru had the most incredible urge to smooth back those strands. Just as he lifted his hand, she looked at him. Her smile had transformed her. What was it Taylor had said? Was he afraid he'd look at Sasha one day and instead of a plain, dour comrade see a beautiful, vibrant woman? Oh, God, it was happening! Sans any love potion whipped up by Granny.

The smile faded, but her face was still aglow with it as her gaze met Tru's. No longer able to repress the urge, he very gently smoothed back those curls that were the color of wheat, from her tawny, silky cheeks.

Despite her concerned efforts, Sasha's heart raced. The best she could do was stand very still and look remote. It wasn't easy.

"So you think I'm argumentative," he murmured.

"I think . . . yes." She forced herself to meet his gaze evenly. All the while her mind, like her heart, was racing. *I must not again be seduced by foolish romanticism*, she told herself over and over.

His gaze dropped from her mesmerizing aquamarine eyes to her equally compelling full lips, which were devoid of lipstick.

Sasha's gaze moved to Tru's mouth.

His lips parted.

Sasha could recognize all the warning signs and yet her lips parted, too. In slow motion, his mouth moved toward hers. When their lips were only a fraction of an inch apart, Sasha wavered. Here was her opportunity to ply her speech about the perils to the mind, soul and body of false sentimentality. Did she not know better than most the dangers incurred when one recklessly unleashed one's emotions? Was she so much like her grandmother that, even having been once demoralized, she would again take the risk? But still she said nothing, made no move. Her breath seemed held by some invisible force when his mouth moved over hers for a whisper-light kiss.

"Was that argumentative?" he murmured.

A shimmer of a smile curved her still-parted lips. "I find no argument with it," she found herself saying when she truly meant to say something quite different, something quite perfunctory.

Tru very much wanted to kiss her again. He sensed that she wouldn't argue against a repeat performance, even one more zealously acted. But an attack of self-preservation held him back. He knew that he was at one of those critical moments in his life that could alter all succeeding ones.

He drew back, staring down at the rich brown freshly tilled soil. It had taken strength and determination to do so thorough a job. But then he had no doubt about Sasha Malzeva Cheeseman's strength and determination. It was his own that he'd just put into serious question.

"I'm sure she'll take you tomorrow," he muttered.

Sasha, far more distracted and disturbed by that brief moment of intimacy than her appearance showed, gave him a puzzled look. "Excuse me?"

"My grandmother. To the shamus. He's good. The family used him once before. Maybe you'll have some luck." As he stepped back, he stumbled on a mound of dirt. He nearly lost his balance but managed to right himself before Sasha could reach out to steady him. He was nervous about her touch at the moment. He was feeling vulnerable, uneasy. Yes. Very uneasy.

Sasha, much to Tru's consternation, seemed completely unruffled. If anything, he suspected she was mildly amused. He added irritation to his other emotions. "Sorry, comrade, I was out of line," he said.

She gave him a blank look.

"I shouldn't have kissed you," he muttered, more unnerved by having to translate.

Ah, here was her chance to reestablish her equilibrium. "I didn't mind," she said nonchalantly.

"Well, you . . . you should have minded," he said peevishly. "You're a . . . married woman."

His obvious disturbance over the kiss helped Sasha to gain more control over her own disturbance. "It was only a little kiss, Tru. A very little kiss. Not a very passionate one. I think maybe you watch too many Hollywood films. You believe you are all heartthrobs, yes? You Americans, I think, make too much of romantic foolishness."

Tru was steaming. "We make too much of it? Well, my dear Mrs. Sasha Malzeva Cheeseman, may I remind you that it was not one of us *Americans* that got swept off her feet and lost her head over a man she didn't know for beans and ended up marrying him two weeks later."

He fully expected either a slap on the face or a rush of tears from Sasha for his crass, insensitive attack. But then he was beginning to learn that Sasha couldn't be counted on to do the expected. Here she was, smiling again.

She may have been smiling on the outside, but she was boiling on the inside. However, she hadn't towed the party line all these years not to know when it was more effective to hold her temper. Yes, let Tru be the foolish one, ranting and raving. She would establish the much-needed upper hand by remaining cool and superior. "So, you give me another good lesson in proper American slang, Tru. 'Don't know for beans?' I must add that expression to my list." She nodded slowly, as if Tru was merely her tutor and she was committing his lesson to memory. But then her smile faded, her mouth set again as she met his hardened gaze. "You are right, Tru," she conceded. "I did not know this man who is my husband for...beans. It is a lot of nonsense—romance. I knew this before. Now, I know it better."

She dropped to her knees. For an instant Tru thought she was faint. But then he saw that she had merely resumed her gardening. He stood there watching her, at a loss for words, and yet feeling like a heel.

"Sasha."

She looked up, her expression muted. "Yes, Tru?"

But he had no follow-up. He had to grab one from thin air. "What . . . kind of vegetables?"

"Turnips, radishes, peas, squash . . . beans." She dropped her gaze.

Tru felt another stab of guilt. "Sasha."

Again she looked up, calm, composed, with an air of detachment that disturbed him far more than it should.

"You do not like these vegetables?" she asked blandly.

"No. Yes." He emitted a dry laugh. "Listen, why don't you leave the vegetables for now and...I'll drive you into town to see Del Monte," he mumbled with what he felt was clumsy gallantry.

"Del Monte?"

"The shamus. The private investigator."

Slowly Sasha rose, dusting the dirt off her hands. She gave him one of her direct, clear-eyed looks, but there was something behind her eyes, a quality that eluded him yet made him feel awkward, uncertain and, damn it, aroused. "You will do that for me? You do not have to go to work today?"

Tru felt heat sting his cheeks. "I'm the president of the company. I can take a . . . morning off. You want to get rolling on this, don't you?"

"Get rolling?"

"Get a jump start. Get a move on. Get going," he said impatiently. "Do you want to plant beans, Mrs. Cheeseman, or do you want to track down this husband of yours?"

Her smile unnerved him more. "I am not arguing with you, Tru. I want very much to get rolling, get a move on. We will step on it, yes?"

Despite himself, his gaze fixed for a lingering moment on her parted, smiling lips. Then, quickly, in a failed attempt to banish his almost-uncontrollable urge to kiss her again, he turned away. "Yes. We should step on it. I'll clean up and meet you in front of your grandmother's house in twenty minutes."

HE'D CHANGED HIS CLOTHES, putting on a pair of freshly laundered black jeans and a turquoise jersey with a lived-in look but seams that were intact. He'd debated about shaving, but decided against it in the end, not wanting Sasha to think that he'd gotten especially spruced up for their little outing. After all, it was strictly business, he told himself, and added for good measure that the sooner she got a lead on her husband, the sooner he'd be rid of her.

He was running a few minutes late and fully expected to find the supremely disciplined and, no doubt, punctual Sasha waiting impatiently for him when he arrived. But when he pulled up on his motorcycle in front of his grandmother's house, she wasn't there. Not envisioning her as the type to be primping and fussing with her appearance, he went inside to see if something was wrong. Maybe his grandmother had returned and taken Sasha into town to see Del Monte herself.

"Sasha!" he called out from the foot of the wide, curving staircase.

Jessica's housekeeper popped her head out of the sitting room, dust mop in hand. "She's up in her room."

Tru hesitated, then took the stairs two at a time. He knocked on the door of the guest room where Sasha was staying.

"Sasha? Anything wrong?"

"I am not sure," came her muffled voice from inside.

"Can I . . . help?"

Slowly, the door opened. At first he almost didn't recognize her. He scowled in disbelief at an ethereal vision of loveliness in a peachy wisp of a sundress, with a matching peach silk scarf worn pirate-fashion on her head, her loose waves of wheat-gold hair falling around her shoulders.

"It is impossible, yes?"

"Yes," he murmured, dumbfounded. And then, seeing the despair in her aquamarine eyes, he quickly amended his one-word response. "I mean, it's impossible to believe how . . . different you look."

"You mean, ridiculous." She started to pull off the silk head wrap, but Tru grabbed her wrist.

"No, not ridiculous at all." He smiled at her. "You look...fine, Sasha. Very...stylish. And here I was thinking the Russians were behind the times in fashion."

"Oh, it is not Russian fashion. It is your grandmother's doing." She held up a page torn from a fashion magazine that featured a model in the exact outfit Sasha was wearing. The model was billed as The Fortune Girl. The layout was a clothing ad for his stores.

Tru's eyes strayed to the bed where he saw an open Fortune's box, the tissue paper neatly folded beside it.

"I find it here when I come in to change," Sasha said. "With note." She handed the note over to Tru. It was very brief. "When in Rome . . ."

"I think, perhaps, your grandmother is not happy with my appearance." Her eyes searched his face for confirmation. Besides looking incredibly beautiful, for the first time Sasha Malzeva Cheeseman looked very young and very vulnerable. Now he remembered his grandmother remarking that she was only twenty-four. Somehow, until this moment, she'd seemed to him to be much older.

He set the fashion page and the note on a nearby bureau and took hold of both of Sasha's hands. He fixed his gaze on her. "This dress is you, Sasha."

"I do not look...foolish?"

He smiled tenderly. "If I saw this dress in a shop window I'd rush you inside, introduce you and say that you were meant for each other."

She only looked at him without speaking.

"Do you understand what I'm saying, Sasha?"

The smile was slow in coming to her lips, but when it did it was heart-stopping. "You are not always so argumentative, Tru. Sometimes, you are very sweet, yes?"

His hands slid up her arms to her shoulders. "*Sweet* is not a word women use very often to describe me."

"Maybe," she murmured, knowing she was only asking for trouble, "you do not know the right women."

Tru knew he was going to kiss her again. He knew that this time there would be no restraint about it. And he knew, as sure as hell as he was breathing, that he was taking one of those irretrievable steps over the line. What he didn't know was that Sasha was thinking precisely the same thing.

His hands encircled her neck, slipping under the luxuriant weight of her hair. "Sasha, Sasha," he whispered.

"You repeat yourself, Tru."

"Exactly."

They tumbled into the kiss together, Sasha's silken head-wrap falling to the floor as Tru's mouth came down hard on hers. He drew her against him. Her arms encircled him and she kissed him back with equal vehemence. For both, it was as though a spring had been released in them so that their kiss was flooded with urgency, almost desperation.

He saw she was flushed when he released her. His gaze moved instinctively to her bed, then returned to her face.

Sasha had no trouble understanding what was on his mind: the universal language of love—or at least passion. For a moment, she was sorely tempted. But it was a flood of temptation that brought her up short; she remembered all too well and all too unhappily feeling that sensation before. She drew back, desperate for some distance, and fixed an expression of benign amusement on her face. "You forget, Tru. I am a married woman."

Tru closed his eyes for a moment and took in a much-needed steadying breath. Damn it, his grandmother had snuck in that love potion after all. He just hadn't expected it would be peach colored and have a six-hundred-dollar price tag hanging from it.

HE DIDN'T REALLY WANT TO go in with her to see Del Monte, but he knew there might be some language barriers even though her English was really quite remarkable. The private eye was likely to use slang that she surely wouldn't understand.

Sasha, still wearing the peach sundress, had forgone the head wrap and wore her hair in her more typical drawn-back style. Tru was disturbed to find that the contrast only seemed to heighten her appeal. She sat stiffly and silently beside him on the solitary bench in the cramped waiting room where a pretty redheaded receptionist kept sneaking him come-hither looks from behind her cluttered desk. Tru smiled over at her a few times, even though he wasn't the least bit interested. He knew he was merely trying to assure Sasha as well as himself that their brief interlude up in her bedroom had no great significance. The problem was, he wasn't feeling assured. And Sasha was either oblivious to the subtle flirtation or she just couldn't care less. This attitude only served to irritate Tru. Romantic foolishness, indeed!

Sasha was well aware of the flirtatious interplay. And it wasn't true that she couldn't care less. It did, however, help to remind her that American men—especially that breed of American men who were virile and attractive and knew wealth and privilege—were not to be trusted. All right, she had let her guard slip for a moment. There was nothing she could do about that. There was no point in endlessly berating herself. She would simply stay on guard and "tow the line" from this point on.

"You can go in now."

Tru jumped at the sound of the receptionist's voice. What surprised him was that Sasha jumped also. So, his comrade wasn't nearly as cool and supremely composed as she appeared. Tru felt a little better.

Victor Del Monte waited for the pair at his open door. Sasha shot Tru a rueful look as they rose from the bench. "This is the shamus?" she whispered.

Tru nodded.

"He is not Humphrey Bogart," she muttered dryly.

Tru smiled. To say that Victor Del Monte didn't look like the tough, macho, seedy Bogie in one of his shamus roles was a vast understatement. Del Monte—a thin, wiry, balding fellow with oversize tortoiseshell glasses and a snappy red bow tie—looked more like an aging computer whiz than a shamus. And his ebullient manner reminded Tru of an insurance salesman.

"Come in. Come in. Always glad to be of service to the Fortune family," Del Monte began effusively, giving Tru a solid pat on the arm and smiling brightly at Sasha as he ushered them inside.

"Did a job for your brother Adam about a year or so back," Del Monte said, with a wink. "That was a case, all right," he added glancing again at Sasha. "Came in all worked up, wanting to find a missing person. A real looker with amnesia."

Del Monte gave Tru a quizzical look. "Never did figure out why your brother Pete showed up after Adam left and encouraged me not to find her too fast. Especially as I read in the papers, not long after, that Adam tracked her down himself and the two of them got hitched. Hey, and then Pete goes and gets hitched, too. I don't get it. You'd think with that tontine hanging over your heads, none of you Fortune boys would go strolling down the aisle. Say, you two aren't—"

"No," Tru said sharply. "She's already married."

Sasha raised one eyebrow. "Yes, one husband too many."

Del Monte glanced at Tru as if to ask, *Is she joking?*

Sasha, not one to waste time, gave the investigator a brief rundown of her situation and then extracted the wedding photo. Del Monte studied it thoughtfully. Then, gazing back up at the pair, he tapped the photo. "I'll tell you something. That face looks familiar. Can't place it yet, but give me a few days, let me do some digging."

"Time is of vital importance to me," Sasha said severely. "I must find him as soon as possible."

"It sounds like this guy might not want to be found," Del Monte pointed out.

"If you do not believe you are capable of handling this assignment..." she replied, but the private eye waved her off.

"No problem. You've come to the right place. I'll get right on this and, like I say, I'll be in touch within a few days."

As they were leaving, with Sasha already out the door, Del Monte caught hold of Tru and drew him inside.

"Now, just to have everything straight, you do really want me to find this guy, right? I mean... This isn't another one of those deals where I—"

"No deals," Tru said firmly. "We want you to do everything possible to trace this man. And we want you to do it as quickly as possible. I guarantee you, Del Monte, no one from my family will be popping in later to tell you to stick this case on a back burner."

IT WAS HOT AND HUMID when they stepped outside. Tru spotted an air-conditioned bar across the street from Del Monte's office and asked Sasha if she wanted a drink.

She didn't answer right away, but her gaze, too, was fixed in that direction. However, she was staring at a middle-aged man in a cheap black suit, who was smoking a cigarette and reading a tabloid as he leaned casually against the bar window.

"Sasha?"

She nodded imperceptibly and a few minutes later they were settled into a booth in the cool, quiet bar, ordering vodkas straight up.

"Are you a big vodka drinker?" Tru asked her.

"No. Only special times. Vodka is expensive." She pronounced it "wodka." "And too much makes my head..." She searched for the word, but couldn't find it.

"Spin?" Tru offered, twirling his index finger.

Sasha smiled. "Yes. Makes my head...spin." Then she looked around the bar.

There he was—the man in the cheap black suit. Sitting on one of the bar stools, a bottle of beer in front of him. He was still reading, still smoking. She didn't think she had ever seen this man before, but his presence gave her an uneasy feeling. Perhaps it was just paranoia—a result of having discovered her husband was a smuggler who had meant to use her as a decoy. Such a revelation was bound to affect her nerves. It could even explain those few reckless moments with Tru up in her room earlier that day.

Tru followed Sasha's gaze. "I can't believe he's your type."

She gave Tru a startled look. "My type? Never."

"What's the attraction, then?"

Sasha merely shrugged, turning her attention fully on Tru, dismissing the stranger from her mind for the moment. "So, are you a big vodka drinker?"

He grinned. "No. I don't usually drink vodka. Just at special times."

Sasha arched a brow. "It is not too expensive for you, I think. You are very rich, yes?" she asked with unabashed directness.

"Well . . . yes, but . . ." Tru paused, then smiled. "But, I have high ideals, comrade, and I always put my money where my mouth is."

They both fell into silence. And though Sasha had averted her gaze from the man on the barstool, she still felt his presence. She focused on Tru instead, who was quietly looking over at her.

"A penny for your thoughts," she said.

"Is that a Russian expression, too?"

"No, but one I've heard Americans say." Drew, for one. "If you are rich I should say, one dollar for your thoughts?"

Tru laughed. "No. A penny will do."

She actually dug into her small purse and produced one, setting it on the table in front of him. He stared down at it. "I'm thinking," he said in a strained voice, "does only vodka make Sasha Malzeva Cheeseman's head spin?"

The waitress arrived with their drinks. To Tru's amazement Sasha downed hers in one neat swallow. The waitress hadn't even left yet.

"Another?" the waitress asked with a surprised smile.

Sasha nodded perfunctorily. When the waitress left, she couldn't quite meet Tru's gaze. "No, it is not the only thing," she muttered.

Tru observed the play of emotions on her face. She leaned back against the green plastic padded booth.

They were both quiet. The silence stretched. Sasha noted that the man at the bar was on his second beer. Just a regular customer, she told herself, but his presence continued to make her uneasy. Then again, for altogether different reasons, so did Tru's.

Tru got up to play something on the jukebox. Sasha was taken aback to see him pause at the bar right by the man who had attracted her attention, and say something to him. Whatever Tru said, the man merely shrugged in response and went back to reading his tabloid.

When Tru returned, a Beatles ballad filled the room. "You like this kind of music?" he asked.

"This one, yes. Some, no. I do not like loud, screaming rock-and-roll music. Tell me, what did you say to that man?"

"I asked if he knew what time it was."

"Why?"

"To see if he had a Russian accent. But he didn't answer me."

Sasha felt a tightness in her stomach. "You think... You think I am being followed? You think they already know about Drew's activities and believe I am his accomplice?"

Tru didn't know what to think. "Maybe they're looking for him just like you and figure you're the best one to lead them to him." Tru flushed. "Or maybe I've just read too many spy novels . . . like Granny."

She managed a half smile. "Yes, you are probably right." Still, she would have felt better if the man had responded to Tru's question and proved he hadn't an accent.

He smiled encouragingly. "Come on, let's not get morbid. Let's talk about something else."

Sasha gave him a pensive look. *Yes*, she thought. *A good idea*. It wasn't wise to let paranoia cloud her judgment. She thought for a while and then remembered a comment the private investigator had made that had puzzled her. "Tell me, Tru, what does Del Monte mean...when he says there is tontine hanging over your heads? This word... *tontine*—I do not know."

Tru gave her a vague smile. "Oh, it's a long story. Maybe sometime, if there is time, I'll tell you all about it. It's not important."

Sasha's second vodka arrived. Tru's glass was still full. He smiled, lifted it and raised it toward her. "Shall we make a toast?"

He tapped the rim of his glass to hers and smiled. "Here's to getting what you want."

She smiled back, but there was an uneasiness in her smile as her gaze swept over to the beer drinker on the stool for another brief moment before reverting to Tru.

3

"I DON'T KNOW WHY YOU think my buying Sasha a decent dress was being devious," Jessica Fortune said blithely. "The girl has a dreadful wardrobe and I merely thought, since I was going to be squiring her around town—"

"You had no intention of 'squiring' her," Tru retorted, not feeling the least bit blithe.

Jessica offered up an innocent look. "I never once so much as suggested you take Sasha to see Del Monte."

"Well, you couldn't take her. And, by the way, since when have you turned to baby-sitting as a sideline?"

Jessica grinned. "You know how I adore children. Now, if only I had some little ones of my own . . ."

"Don't look at me," Tru warned.

Jessica smiled benignly. "I was thinking about Adam and Eve. And, of course, Peter and Elizabeth, once they settle into married life a bit. Isn't it wonderful to see them all so happy?"

"Well, I'm happy as a lark, myself. Or I would be, if you—"

"What are you up in arms about, Tru? It was your decision to take Sasha to see the private eye today. I told her I'd be happy to take her tomorrow. And, despite what you think, I left off that dress for her to wear when I took her into town." Jessica pretended an interest in the crewel pillow she'd been stitching for months. "She did look lovely in it, didn't she?" she murmured.

Tru glared at his grandmother, but she didn't look up.

"All right," he relented. "She's attractive enough when she makes the effort. Maybe if she'd made more of an effort, her husband wouldn't have walked out on her."

Now Jessica did look up. "Oh, really, Tru. You don't believe for one moment that's the reason. That awful man conned poor Sasha. And I must say, I'm surprised he was able to pull the wool over her eyes. But then, love can do that to a person." Jessica regarded her crewelwork. "Although I wonder if it was really love. Even in that wedding photo . . . I don't know—they just didn't look right together. And it's obvious that Sasha feels nothing but regret now. And fear."

"Fear? Don't say that to Sasha. She'll deny it vehemently. We're talking one tough cookie here, Gran."

"Yes. But you see it, too, don't you, Tru?"

Tru raised up his hands as if to stop her right there. "I don't want to see anything. I don't want to get involved. I've got a company to run. I'm trying to bring Fortune's into the twenty-first century. I finally have the road clear to institute the kinds of changes I spent years trying to get Dad and then Pete to make. And no woman, even one that's drop-dead beautiful, is going to distract me."

"Drop-dead beautiful?" Jessica mused.

"Oh, you're impossible." He started to leave.

"Only last week you told me you were planning to take a couple of weeks off before the month was out," Jessica remarked, as though Tru weren't in the process of making a dramatic exit. "And I remember wholeheartedly agreeing that you needed a break. After all, since Pete's marriage you've been working practically around the clock. All those changes. Didn't you say yourself, you need to let things percolate awhile, step away from it all and get a clearer perspective about what's working and what isn't?"

"I wouldn't have said one word to you if I knew my words were going to come back to haunt me," Tru muttered. "And if I do decide to take some time off, I'm going to take the company plane and fly up to the mountains for some solitary rock-climbing."

"You have been rather edgy lately, and getting away might do you good."

Tru turned and gave his grandmother a wary look. "If you're plotting another 'chance meeting' for me and Sasha up in the mountains—"

"Really, Tru. You have a most suspicious nature. Which is precisely why I thought you'd be of assistance to Sasha. She was bamboozled once, poor thing...."

"Believe me," Tru argued, "she's not the sort that makes the same mistake twice."

Jessica, however, didn't seem convinced. "Despite what you think or what she says, she shouldn't be allowed to go after this . . . this criminal . . . on her own."

"Well, don't look at me," Tru told her. "I'm going to follow your advice and go off to climb mountains for a week."

"Very well," Jessica said calmly, doing a few more stitches.

Tru hesitated, but finally sat down across from his grandmother. "Listen to me, Granny. Don't go getting any ideas here."

"Ideas?"

"I don't want you thinking you ought to be going off with Sasha to confront this creep. You said yourself, this is a case for the authorities."

"And you heard what Sasha said about that."

"Okay, then. If Del Monte finds out where this guy is, I'll have him see what else he can find out on him. If we can get the goods on him for some other job before or since Sasha, that would pretty much clear her."

"If we could do that—"

"I don't mean *we* meaning *me*. I'll talk to Del Monte before I cut out for the mountains, and then it's in his hands."

"Yes, dear. I understand. It's a very good suggestion. I do worry, though, that if Sasha discovers where her husband is, she's going to be adamant about a face-to-face confrontation. Afraid or not, she's very strong-willed."

"Yes, I know."

"Perhaps you ought to have a talk with her, before you go off on your rock-climbing expedition. You know— impress upon her the risks of being reckless or impulsive."

Tru could feel the heat rising up his collar. Right, he thought. Like he was the one to talk!

IT WAS A LITTLE AFTER eleven that night. Tru was trying to settle down, but he was restless. He started thinking that he could probably clear up a few things at work tomorrow, stop in to have that talk with Del Monte, and leave for the mountains by evening. Yes, that was the thing to do. The sooner the better.

He grabbed a can of beer, stepped out back to his small patio and stretched out on a chaise longue. He tried to relax. He tried not to think about Sasha Malzeva Cheeseman and her problems. He tried especially not to think about the heated kiss they'd shared. He wasn't having much success.

He swallowed some of his beer but that didn't divert him from his treacherous thoughts. Okay, so he was attracted to her. She did look drop-dead beautiful in that peach sundress. So, he'd kissed her. What was the big deal? It was all a bunch of romantic foolishness, just as Sasha had said. As for worrying about her going off half-cocked after her smuggler husband, he'd have a word with Del Monte about keeping the guy's whereabouts to himself until he got the goods on him. Then, if Sasha still wanted a confrontation with the bastard, hopefully there'd be metal bars between them.

SASHA JUST COULDN'T GET comfortable. Certainly there was nothing wrong with the queen-size bed with its fine linen sheets. And there was even a deliciously cool breeze blowing in through the open windows. No. Her restlessness had nothing to do with her surroundings or the weather. Nor did it even have to do with her soon-to-be ex-husband's treachery. What it had solely to do with was Truman Fortune. Here she had lectured him on romance being a lot of nonsense, and now she was once again finding herself caught in its insidious snare. Had she learned nothing from her disastrous union with one American? Was she now embarking on a folly with another one? What was the matter with her? Did she have no common sense, at all?

She flung off the covers and got out of bed. All right, so she found Tru attractive. But she also found him arrogant, argumentative, rude—at times. Yet, at other times . . .

She told herself she was indulging in false sentimentality, that she was letting bourgeois American emotions overwhelm her reason and good judgment. She knew that she had to get a grip on herself. She had come to America with one purpose and one purpose only: to find the bastard who had deceived her and demand that he return with her to Russia to make amends by giving back the icon. If he refused or in any way threatened her, she would warn him that she had left a detailed letter with a good friend in Moscow to be handed over to the authorities if she and her husband didn't return. Sasha greatly hoped she could persuade Drew to cooperate, for both their sakes, since, in truth, no such friend existed.

She threw on a T-shirt and a pair of jeans—American jeans she'd paid an exorbitant price for on the black market in Russia a few weeks before; an impulse purchase, one that she'd chastised herself for afterward. But she did love them....

TRU CAST ASIDE THE half-full beer can. He couldn't sit still. After pacing around for a bit, he finally decided to go for a bike ride out in the countryside.

He was racing down the long winding drive on his Harley a few minutes later when his low beam suddenly illuminated a figure in its path. It was Sasha, strolling down the center of the drive. She had turned in alarm as the light hit her, freezing in place. Tru curved sharply to the right, nearly overturning the bike as he squealed to a stop.

"Are you crazy?" he shouted at her, shaken by the possibility that he could have hit her if he'd been going much faster.

She glared at him. "Am I crazy? I am not the one racing madly down the driveway on a motorcycle in the middle of night."

"I suppose it's less crazy to be out for a stroll in the middle of the night?"

Her hair, which she hadn't bothered to pin back, was blowing all over her face. She drew it back with her hand. "Must you always argue?"

He opened his mouth to do just that, then stopped, grinning instead. "Okay, no more arguments. Get on," he said impulsively.

She hesitated. "Where are you going?"

"Must *you* always argue, Sasha?"

"I am not—" She stopped. "Okay. But you must not ride like a Hell's Angel, yes?"

"Yes," he agreed, smiling.

He handed her an extra helmet from his satchel, then helped her fasten it. "I have never ridden on a motorcycle before," she announced solemnly.

Tru touched her cheek. "Don't worry. I'll take it nice and slow."

Their eyes met and held. "I think I should worry, since I do not think you can do that," she murmured.

"I'd say that makes two of us."

THE ROAR OF THE MOTOR and the wind kept conversation to a bare minimum, which suited them both. Sasha held on to Tru, but her grip loosened as she grew more confident. Actually, she found the ride exhilarating and wouldn't have minded if he'd driven a bit faster.

After about forty-five minutes, Tru pulled off at a scenic rest stop. Not that there was much of a vista at close to midnight with clouds obscuring most of the stars. Still, a crescent of moon cast a faint, hazy light over the landscape. Sasha alighted from the bike and perched on top of a picnic table, looking out at the eerie view. A moment later, Tru joined her.

"It is very beautiful, your country," she murmured.

"I'll have to show you this spot during the day sometime. It's one of my favorites." As soon as the words were
out, he regretted them. What was he doing, making dates
with Sasha? "Listen. I'm . . . going out of town . . . for a
while."

"Yes?" she said in that smoky voice, her one-word response offering him no clue to her reaction to his state-
ment.

She continued looking straight ahead as Tru glanced
at her profile, which was a fascinating blend of light
planes and dark shadows. "A much-needed vacation,"
he added emphatically.

She merely nodded.

"I'm sure Del Monte will dig something up
on . . . Cheeseman. Maybe more than you even suspect."

"What do you mean?"

"Sasha, this probably wasn't the creep's first outing.
Maybe he's been smuggling stuff in from Russia and who
knows where else for years. Maybe he's even part of some
sort of network."

"Network?"

"A big-time smuggling operation. Look, it's even possible that this Cheeseman's got a dozen aliases with
phony passports to match and it'll be impossible to track
him down. Maybe you ought to just go back to Moscow, and forget about it."

"You think I can forget?"

Tru gazed at her ruefully. "No, I don't suppose you
can."

"I do not find it pleasant to believe he is a longtime
master criminal. My hope is that this is not the case, that
this was his first time. And that he will return with me
and set things right."

"And then?"

"We will get a proper Russian divorce."

"Even if he sets things right and he's really sorry for what he did? What if he wants to . . . try to work things out between you?"

"It is too late," she said without hesitation.

"There is some slim possibility you've got the guy all wrong, you know. What if that icon was planted on him? What if he doesn't even know anything about it?"

Sasha gave him a doubtful look.

"Okay, it's a reach, but it's possible."

"Then why did he lie to me? Why did he vanish?"

"I don't know," Tru admitted. "Maybe he was in some kind of danger and got away to protect your life. Have you thought of that possibility?"

"No."

"Or that someone planted the goods on him."

"I do think you read too many spy books."

He was about to argue, but instead he laughed. "I think you're probably right."

She smiled ever so faintly. "At last we agree."

He observed her closely. "You should do that more often."

She was immediately guarded. "Do what?"

"Smile."

"Why?" she asked soberly, all trace of the smile gone.

"Why? Because . . . it feels good, it . . . looks good, it . . . makes other people smile back."

"What are we smiling about?"

"What kind of a question is that? I don't know specifically what we're supposed to be smiling about."

"Neither do I," she replied matter-of-factly.

He sighed with frustration. "You're right. What do we have to be smiling about, anyway?"

"Exactly."

There was a long silence.

"I'm just curious," Tru finally said. "Does anything at all ever just amuse you, Sasha?"

"Amuse me?"

"You know. Make you laugh? A deep belly laugh? Like when you hear a really funny joke?"

Sasha gave him a blank look. "What joke?"

Tru scowled and then turned pensive. For some inexplicable reason he felt compelled to make Sasha laugh. Just once. Just to see how she would look. Just to break through that staunch seriousness. It would do her good. Hell, it would do them both good.

He rubbed his jaw, trying to recall some of the jokes he'd heard at work. "Let's see. Okay, I have one. This extremely tall man with round shoulders, very long arms, and one leg six inches shorter than the other went into a tailor's shop—"

"Why is this man so misshapen?"

"I don't know. That's not the point. So . . . where was I? Okay, so he goes into the tailor shop, see, and he says to the tailor—"

"Perhaps he was in the war."

Tru was losing his patience. "Will you stop thinking about why he's— Okay, forget it. Maybe that's not such a good joke." He paused for a minute, while Sasha waited silently.

"Okay," he said finally. "Here's a better one. There were these two Irishmen who bought two horses at a fair. But both of the horses—"

"Why Irishmen?"

Tru scowled. "They don't have to be Irishmen. They can be Italians. They can be Scandinavians. They can be...Russians. Okay, if that'll make you happier, they're Russians. The point is they bought these two horses."

"Yes. Very well," Sasha said complacently.

Tru eyed her for several moments before going on. "This happens to be a funny joke. When I heard it the first time I laughed my head off. When I heard the punch line, that is. Which I'm trying to get to."

He scratched the side of his nose. "Okay. So the thing was these two horses looked a lot alike, so Pat says to Mike—"

"Pat and Mike?"

"Yes. Pat and Mike. Is there something wrong with that?"

"I know no Russians with the names Pat and Mike."

Tru waved an accusing finger at her. "You're doing it deliberately."

Sasha shrugged. "I am only saying—"

"Never mind. Forget it."

Sasha faintly smiled. "You are angry?"

"No."

"You do not want to tell me the joke now?"

"I realize you probably won't think it's funny anyway. It was a bad idea. Let's just forget it. Drop the whole thing."

There was another long silence.

"So, you go on vacation tomorrow?" Sasha asked.

"What?" Tru had forgotten all about the vacation. "Oh. Yes. Well...late in the day. If I can tie up all the loose ends at work. Maybe the day after. Or by weekend."

"You will go with a friend?"

"No. No friend."

"You are not . . . lonely?" Her smoky voice sounded rough around the edges.

"No," Tru said after a pause.

"But you will have no one to smile for, no one to smile for you."

He gave her a rueful look. "Sometimes that's just as well."

There was a sudden gust of wind. Tru looked up at the sky. The clouds had solidified, almost obscuring the moon entirely now. It seemed likely that it would rain. Riding a bike through a storm along these winding mountain roads would be risky. *Best not to take any unnecessary chances*, he told himself, knowing he was worrying about more than the rain.

They hadn't gone far when the rain started. Tru estimated they were still a good twenty miles from home. If the rain picked up they'd have to seek shelter.

Within minutes, the storm came in earnest. "We've got to find some cover," he shouted back to Sasha, who was now very wet and clinging tightly to him.

Visibility was practically nil as they pulled over to the side of the road. Neither of them was dressed for a storm; their thin clothes were soaked and pressing against their skin.

"Look," Sasha said, pointing to a faintly flickering light a short distance ahead. Tru laced his hand with hers and they made a run for it.

The light was coming from one of a group of small cabins in a clearing in the woods not far from the road. Over the solitary bulb outside the door of the cabin was a sign: No Vacancy.

As they huddled under the stingy metal canopy, Tru wiped the rain from his face and looked around. "I don't see any cars parked at a couple of the cabins and it's well after midnight. Maybe the manager just didn't want to be awakened in the middle of the night if a weary traveler came along."

"You will wake him, then?" Sasha asked, her voice quivery as a chill shot through her.

Tru put an arm around her shoulder. "No. Come on. Let's see if we can get into one of the unoccupied cabins and I'll settle up in the morning."

He started to make a run for it, only to have Sasha yank him back. "It is against the law, yes? We can be arrested."

"There are extenuating circumstances, Sasha. You won't get into trouble, I promise you. If we stand out here arguing much longer, we're both going to come down with pneumonia."

"Pneumonia is bad, but prison—"

"This isn't a criminal offense. Exactly." He sighed. "Okay. Wait. I have an idea." He pulled his wet billfold out of his back pocket and extracted three twenty-dollar bills. "This will more than cover the cost of a cabin for the night." He bent down and slid the bills under the office door.

Sasha was still a little leery, but she was also cold and wet, so she raced with Tru to an empty cabin about fifty yards away. The front door was locked, but he managed, much to Sasha's consternation, to jimmy open a window.

Tru motioned Sasha to climb in. Impulsively, he gave her a soft kiss. He told himself it was merely to reassure her, but he'd never been good at lying to himself.

Her lips tingling, Sasha felt more nervous than ever about climbing into the cabin, only now it had less to do with getting caught by the authorities and being deported than it did finding herself alone for the night in a desolate cabin with this impossibly attractive man. She hoped there were at best two separate rooms, or, at the very least, two separate beds.

But there was only one room, one bed. The bedraggled pair stared at it in awkward silence. The silence was broken by Sasha's sneeze. "You've got to get out of those wet things."

Sasha nodded, observing him. "You, too."

Tru nodded. Another awkward silence ensued. They both looked around the sparsely furnished one-room cabin. Tru crossed over to the door that led into a tiny, drab bathroom. He flicked on the light switch, then glanced back at the shivering Sasha. "Why don't you—uh—get undressed in there and take a nice hot shower."

"You must shower, too."

Just for a moment there, he was tempted to toss out the line, Save Water. Shower With A Friend. He fought the urge. Instead, he said, "After you," with forced gallantry.

Sasha nodded, starting for the bathroom. Tru was still standing at the bathroom door. She slipped inside and was about to close the door, when Tru called out, "Wait."

Sasha felt a jolt of nervousness until she saw him hurry over to the bed and pull off the solitary blanket, bringing it over to her. "Here. You'll need to wrap yourself up in something when you're done. By morning our clothes should be dry."

She took the blanket, compressing her lips as she stared down at it. "And you?"

"Me?"

She glanced at the bed where now only a top sheet remained. Tru followed her gaze. "Oh, I'll make do with the sheet. Don't worry."

She was again about to close the door when Tru added, "You can have the bed. I'll—uh—pull the two chairs together."

Sasha stared dubiously at the two rickety wooden chairs that were on either side of an equally rickety-looking table at the far end of the room.

"It's fine, really. I like roughing it once in a while." To stem any arguments, he grabbed the knob of the bathroom door and shut her inside.

A couple of minutes later he heard the shower going. Trying to fend off disturbing erotic visions of a naked Sasha under the steamy spray, Tru stripped out of his sodden clothes. Finding no extra blanket anywhere in the room, he wrapped the top sheet from the bed toga-fashion around his damp, naked body. He had barely gotten the makeshift wrap adjusted when the shower went off. A minute later, Sasha emerged. When she sighted Tru, she smiled. "You look like Caesar, yes?"

Tru felt more like a Caesar salad, looking at her, all dewy fresh from the shower, a pink flush highlighting her cheeks, her towel-dried hair falling in abandon around her shoulders, wearing only the thin blanket and that incredible smile she was so stingy with.

Her smile faded as she saw his somber expression. "I hope I did not use all of the hot water."

Tru smiled then. "I'm sure you didn't. In fact you might have set the record for the fastest shower of any woman in America. Certainly you beat out every woman I know." He flushed. "I mean . . ."

"I know what you mean, Tru." Her eyes sparkled.

Tru hurried into the bathroom to shower. A cold shower!

When he stepped out a few minutes later, he saw Sasha rigidly lying as far over to one side of the double bed as she could, the blanket spread neatly over the whole bed, a bit less than half of it over herself. Without looking at him, she mumbled, "We must not be foolish. There is one bed. We are two people. So, we will not make a large deal of this situation, yes?"

Tru was completely thrown off guard. "Yes. I mean . . . no." As tempting as the idea might be of crawling into bed beside Sasha, it was just too damn risky.

"No, that's okay. I'm perfectly happy with the chairs."

Sasha felt a mix of relief and disappointment. "As you like."

Tru set the two chairs facing each other.

"There," he said, settling onto one of the chairs and propping his feet up on the other. His knees buckled in the middle.

"Perhaps it would be more comfortable if you placed your chairs farther apart," Sasha suggested politely.

Tru was not in the mood for suggestions. "This is fine."

"Yes?"

"I'll sleep like a baby," he lied, trying to find a comfortable position. He readjusted himself and his draped sheet several times. Finally, he came up with the solution of tipping the chair he was sitting in back a little.

"There," he said. "That's perfect." He stretched out his legs now, not realizing, until too late, that the movement would angle his chair just far enough back to tip it—and him—right over. The next thing he knew, he was flat on his back, with one foot sticking up in the air, the other caught in between two rungs of a chair.

For a moment, when he saw her face screw up, he thought she was about to cry in alarm. But the next moment, to his irritation, she burst into laughter.

"So this is what you find amusing?" Tru snapped as he tried to untangle himself from the chairs and hold on to his sheet at the same time, all of which only made Sasha laugh harder. She knew he was embarrassed and annoyed with her, and she tried to stop, even flattening her palm against her mouth, but her laughter broke through. Deep belly laughs. Just the sort Tru had thought were an impossibility for her.

When he was finally on his feet, his sheet once more secure around him, Tru simply glared at her.

"Oh, I—am—sorry," she said, between laughs. "You aren't—hurt?"

"No, I'm not. And no, you aren't sorry. You have a perverse sense of humor, that's what."

But as he continued watching her laugh, his anger dissipated. And a moment later, he found himself laughing heartily with her.

"YOU HAVE ENOUGH BLANKET?"

Tru was as close to the far side of the bed as was humanly possible without falling off. "Yes. More than enough."

Sasha lay stiffly on her back, eyes open, staring up at the ceiling in the dark. She had never been able to sleep on her back, but she felt awkward about rolling over onto her side.

"Do you have enough blanket?" Tru asked after a long silence.

"Oh, yes," Sasha said quickly.

"And . . . enough . . . space?"

"Oh, yes. Plenty. In Russia, beds are not so big."

"Really?"

"Oh, yes. They are . . . smaller."

"You mean narrower?"

"That, too."

Silence.

"Well, we should get some sleep. It's late."

"Yes."

"Good night, Sasha."

"Good night, Tru."

Neither of them closed their eyes. Both doubted they would be able to sleep a wink all night. Unless . . .

Neither of them allowed themselves to finish that thought.

"Are you still awake?" he asked after about an hour.

"No," she said alertly.

He smiled. "I thought so."

They were separated from each other by a foot of cloth.

He looked over at her. In the murky darkness he could just make out her profile. His desire was merely reflex. Being in bed with a woman—a young woman; all right, a very desirable woman—what else could he expect? But it would be pure insanity to make a move. First, she'd surely rebuff him, which would be a definite bruise to his ego. And if she didn't rebuff him, they'd be crossing that line of no return. Too risky. Far too dangerous.

Even as these thoughts spun through his mind, his body edged closer to hers. He could hear her breathing change. Her body heat seemed to radiate toward him, drawing him still closer.

"Sasha," he whispered hoarsely.

She turned her head to him. Even in the darkness her aquamarine eyes seemed to glitter. Her lips parted. They were so close, but not yet touching. Slowly, Tru's hand moved to her mouth. Her lips captured his fingers. That moment of contact took them both past any thought of stopping what was surely fate.

He leaned over her, kissing her mouth, his fingers splayed over her face. A small alarm went off inside her head, but instead of heeding it, Sasha's mind shut it off. *Out of order!* Then a tiny moan escaped her lips and she kissed him back with fiery intensity, her tongue slipping boldly into his mouth.

Her hair cascaded over her shoulders, draping her breasts. Gently, provocatively, Tru swept the damp strands aside with his palms, dipping his head down to catch an already taut nipple between his lips.

"You taste so good," he murmured, slipping his hands down to her hips and then over her firm buttocks, pulling her closer. She trembled and he felt the quiver like a jolt down his own spine.

His hands felt so warm against her flesh. So warm. So good. He was stroking her, caressing her, licking her, and Sasha was submerged in the rhythm of it. His hands, his mouth, his whole body was a narcotic, drugging her, exciting her to the point of giddiness.

Dizzied, she didn't protest as his hot tongue made a delicious trail from her breasts over her stomach, then lower still. He lifted her slightly, arching her, urging her thighs apart, making her sighs flutter like the murmuring of her heart.

He licked her with tantalizing lightness, then with increasing pressure as she began writhing against him. He felt the tensing of her muscles.

She called out his name, unashamedly drawing her legs up and apart even farther. And as shudders rocked through her, she twined her fingers through his hair.

Tru saw tears in her eyes as he moved over her, but she was smiling as she pulled him down over her, so that his length covered hers. Her hand snaked down between their bodies, cupping him, stroking him, guiding him inside her.

"Sasha, Sasha, Sasha," he whispered, kissing her eyes, cheeks, lips, his strokes rising and falling with the rhythmic cry of her name. He felt his heart hammering against his chest with such force he thought it would burst right through his skin. He had never in all his life felt so sexually alive.

"Oh, yes, yes," he said in a thick voice.

Her legs circled his thighs, and her fingertips pressed into the contours of his muscles as he breathed against her ear in fiery gasps. Now both of them were frantic for release. For an instant, just before they tumbled over the edge, Sasha looked up at him, her eyes liquid. "Now," she whispered. "Oh, now . . ."

And in the space of a heartbeat, linked together, they were soaring.

Afterward, their bodies entwined, they did not so much fall asleep as collapse into it.

IN THE LIGHT OF DAY, they both felt more than a little stunned by the intensity of their intimacy of the night before; ashamed of themselves, guilty, awkward. The worst part of all was that they both still felt aroused.

Sasha reached for her jeans, slipped them on under the covers, then slid out of bed, grabbed the rest of her clothes and hurried silently to the bathroom. She stayed in there a long time, grateful not to be disturbed by Tru. She needed time to compose herself.

When she stepped out of the bathroom, Tru was fully dressed. She moved briskly toward him and stopped to face him defiantly.

"This must never happen again," she stated solemnly.

"Never," Tru agreed quickly, resolutely.

There was a momentary silence as they continued to stare at each other.

"We will forget it ever happened," she added.

Tru nodded. "Yes."

Sasha swallowed hard. "Well, perhaps we cannot forget, but we will never . . . speak of it."

Tru ran his fingers across his sealed lips.

Sasha felt her pulse beating overtime. "We must not even . . . think about it."

"Right," Tru said firmly.

Sasha took in a steadying breath. "Perhaps, we will think about it, but what is important is that we never let it . . . happen again."

A glimmer of a smile played on Tru's lips. "I believe you said that already."

Sasha drew her shoulders back and turned to the door. "Perhaps it bears repeating, comrade."

THEY HOPED TO BE ABLE to sneak back home before anyone—especially Jessica—awoke, so that their overnight escapade would go unnoticed and unquestioned. Sasha was merely embarrassed at the prospect of her hostess's all-too-correct presumption that something illicit had gone on between her and Tru. Tru, who was equally concerned about that, was even more concerned that this would add fuel to his grandmother's fire, leading her to believe she had another match in the making.

At close to seven o'clock, when Tru pulled around the circular drive to the front of his grandmother's house to drop Sasha off, he was disconcerted to see an unfamiliar car parked there. For one thing, it meant that his grandmother had probably been awakened. For another, he couldn't imagine who would come calling at such an early hour—and why.

When the front door opened and Victor Del Monte stepped out, Tru got the answer to the "who." And he had a good guess about the "why." As he glanced over at Sasha, he could see that she did, too.

4

SASHA STARED SILENTLY at the newspaper clipping from the *Seattle Monitor* while Jessica stood on one side of her, Tru on the other. They, too, studied the clipping, which included a grainy photograph of a man whose name was listed as Martin Baker, a thirty-seven-year-old Seattle travel agent who died from stab wounds after being attacked by a mugger while jogging in a Seattle park two evenings ago.

Del Monte fingered his bow tie. "Is that Cheeseman? Sure as hell looks like the guy in the wedding photo you left with me."

Sasha looked up slowly, her face expressionless. "Yes, this is Drew."

"You're sure?" Jessica questioned. "It could be someone who resembles him—"

"I am sure," Sasha said, her voice giving no clue to her emotions. Her gaze fell on the clipping again. "Today is Tuesday, yes?"

"Yes," Tru replied gently.

She nodded. Jessica lightly touched Sasha's shoulder. "This must be quite a shock, my dear. Come, sit down. Have you eaten?" She took in Tru as well as Sasha, noting their still slightly damp, rumpled attire.

"We—uh—went out for a ride on the Harley last night and got caught in a storm," Tru felt compelled to explain. "Had to hole up for a few hours." He omitted any details.

Jessica took in the information with a seemingly bland nod. "Then nice hot showers are in order for both of you. I'll see about your breakfast while you're changing."

"I must go," Sasha said abruptly.

"Go? Go where, my dear? Back to Moscow? Yes, of course, I understand you would want to go home now, but not immediately," Jessica soothed. "You mustn't rush off. You've had quite a shock. It will take time—"

"I have no time. It is today," Sasha insisted.

Tru shot his grandmother a glance, then focused on Sasha. "What's today?"

"The funeral," Sasha explained. "It says here a funeral will be held for Martin Baker at three o'clock at the First Presbyterian Church on Wilmott Street in Seattle."

SASHA WAS PACKING her few items of clothing in her worn satchel up in the guest room as Jessica continued to try to dissuade her from going to Seattle.

"What purpose will it serve?" she asked.

"Purpose?" Sasha paused. "I do not know. I feel that I have so few answers about this man. I marry a Drew Cheeseman who I believe sells farm machinery in Chicago. Then he vanishes and I find this icon hidden away in his belongings and I do not know what to think. Is he a smuggler? Was I to be nothing more than his unwitting accomplice? Could there be some other explanation? Now, he can give me no explanations, no help. Now, a man by the name of Martin Baker is dead—stabbed to death...."

Jessica placed her hand over Sasha's. "Maybe it is best to leave it be, my dear. Whatever questions you are left with, I doubt you will find the answers in Seattle."

"I must try. I will also need the death certificate to bring back to Moscow so that I can be classified a . . . widow by my government."

"I can arrange for the certificate," Jessica offered.

Sasha smiled wearily at Jessica. "You understand it is more than that." She carefully folded a plain white blouse. "Perhaps somebody there—somebody else at the funeral—also knew a man named Drew Cheeseman."

"If that is the case, this somebody might have been involved in . . . nefarious activities with him. It could be very dangerous for you."

Sasha continued packing. "I appreciate your concern, Jessica, but I assure you I am very well able to look after myself. And if others are involved, it will only help my position to find them and have them brought to justice. Surely then, my government will realize I was not acting in . . ."

"Cahoots?" Jessica suggested.

"Yes," Sasha agreed solemnly. "Precisely."

Jessica frowned. "All the more reason not to be in Seattle on your own. I'm sure, if you asked Tru, he would go with you. It would be better to have someone—"

"No. Tru must not come with me. It is best for me to go alone. This is not his problem. I am not his problem."

"Did anything happen between you last night—"

Sasha flushed. "Believe me, Jessica, your grandson behaved admirably. What is it you say in America? He was a perfect gentleman." She looked away. Lying did not come easily to her.

Jessica smiled. "I wasn't inquiring about...that. I only wondered if you two had argued, had words."

"We did not argue." Sasha thought back to their night together in the cabin. She thought about how he had finally made her laugh; how silly she'd felt, laughing like that—how good it had felt. And she thought about lying in bed beside him, trying so desperately to fight that current of attraction that vibrated through her. But she could not fight it. Nor could Tru. What was it about American men? But even as that thought crossed her mind, she knew she couldn't so easily toss Tru into a category. Tru was unique. Tru made her feel more than physically alive. She sighed inwardly. It was good she had a plane to catch.

She caught Jessica watching her cannily. Sasha was reminded of her own shrewd grandmother, who somehow always managed to see through her facade to the inner turmoil she so often struggled against.

"I wonder," Jessica said after a moment. "Has Tru told you about the tontine yet?"

Sasha gave her a curious look. "No," she replied. "The private investigator mentioned it, but when I asked Tru what this meant—a tontine—he told me it was not important."

Sasha was surprised to see Jessica smile. And her next words surprised her even more. "Well, isn't that curious?" Jessica mused.

"I don't understand."

"Tru's first defense is always to tell every new woman he meets about the tontine. It's his safety net."

"Safety net?" Sasha, for all her expert knowledge of the English language, was having difficulty following.

Jessica merely smiled, and before Sasha could inquire further about the tontine, the older woman left the room.

"TRU, YOU CAN'T LET HER go to Seattle by herself," Jessica argued.

"You told me she made it clear she wanted to go alone."

"It could be dangerous. Oh, she acts as though she can handle anything, but I know as well as you do that—"

"She's going to the funeral of a Martin Baker, Gran. It's obvious the guy led a dual life. I'll lay you odds Baker was considered an upstanding member of the community, a quiet, zealous worker who . . . traveled a lot. I'm sure Sasha will be perfectly safe. Anyway. . ." He hesitated, unable to meet her steady, inquisitive gaze.

Jessica observed him quietly, and waited.

"Maybe," he said uneasily, "she really did care about the guy in spite of it all, and wants some. . .time to mourn in private."

Jessica harrumphed. "I grant you she's stunned and understandably upset. But I don't think she's going to mourn his loss. No. I think Sasha's far more her grandmother Leila's kin than she lets on."

"What does that mean?"

"It means," Jessica replied, "that she's an impetuous young woman with a weakness for adventure and risk-taking." She gave Tru a sly look, as if to say she knew someone else who was equally impetuous and had a weakness for adventure and risk-taking.

Tru deliberately ignored that look. Now that he was president of Fortune's and had a vast conglomerate to run, he was determined to temper some of his reckless impulsivity—albeit a little late.

"YOU DID NOT HAVE TO drive me to the airport, Tru," Sasha said stiffly as she sat beside him in the vintage MG sports car he drove when he wasn't on his Harley.

Tru grinned. "Madison would have taken you, but he's under the weather this morning. Something tells me it's a hangover. Besides, the poor old fellow's a little afraid of you."

"I was only trying to give him confidence to—"

"Start a revolution of antiquated American chauffeurs?"

Sasha gave him a sharp look. "He should not have to be a chauffeur at his age."

"Maybe he likes being a chauffeur. Maybe he takes pride in his position and enjoys his work and all the perks that come with it—including a very tidy salary, a pension plan that he can use whenever he chooses to retire, which is entirely up to him. Not to mention a damn nice apartment on the grounds, plenty of time off—"

"Must we argue?"

Tru fell silent. Neither of them spoke for nearly the rest of the drive.

"I hope you don't run into rain," he said innocuously as they neared the airport. "It rains a lot in Seattle."

"In Moscow, too." Then she added softly, "And in Denver."

As he turned into the airport parking lot, he blurted out, "Are you sure you want to do this?"

"Yes," she answered solemnly.

"It could be risky."

"I will be fine."

As was typical on a weekday morning, the terminal was crowded—mostly with business people hurrying about with their carry-on overnighters and attaché cases, and jockeying for position in line at the string of airline check-ins.

Sasha was waiting at the end of a long line in front of the Northwest Airlines counter as Tru came over with a magazine and a couple of candy bars for her. He paused to observe her. She looked very much as she had a few days before when she'd first arrived. Her hair was once again pulled severely back from her face. Again she wore that drab brown skirt and blouse, and those serviceable brown oxfords. The woman should have looked dreadful. But now, for all her attempts at plainness and her lack of stylish clothing, Tru had no difficulty whatsoever seeing through to Sasha's natural beauty and vitality. He had no trouble recalling the vibrant, laughing, sensual woman he'd been with in the cabin last night. Yes, he thought, Jessica was right. Sasha really did resemble her grandmother despite all the superficial evidence to the contrary. He felt a disquieting flash of arousal coupled with an almost-irresistible urge to carry Sasha off to the nearest hotel. . . .

A buxom, middle-aged woman accidentally jammed Tru with her suitcase as she rushed by, jostling him back to his senses. He hurried over to Sasha, anxious to hand her the items he'd purchased and then take off before he started getting any funny ideas.

"It is not necessary," she said as he deposited the magazine and candy bars in her hand.

"The chocolate will give you energy. We didn't get much sleep last night." He could be a master of understatement. Eager to push aside the memory of last night, he tapped the magazine she was now holding. "It's a good one. Lots of jokes inside. Who knows? Maybe you'll begin to get the hang of American humor."

"I mean it is not necessary for you to wait with me. I am fine."

Tru hesitated. All he had to do was agree with her, bid her farewell, and skip out. So what was holding him back? "My grandmother seems to think you might be feeling . . . some grief. Over Cheeseman. Or Baker. Whatever name he went by, he was your husband."

"It was a very short marriage," Sasha said dryly. "Almost as short as the . . . engagement."

They moved up together in the line.

"So you're not a grieving widow?"

Sasha couldn't quite meet his eyes. "I am sad," she admitted. "Like you said, Drew was a charmer. He swept me off my feet. I was dazzled. But that is not love." She hesitated. "And I was . . . never before with an . . . American man." *We will forget it ever happened between us. We will not speak of it. We will not think of it. We must never let it happen again.*

"Was he so different from the Russian men you've been with?" *Why was he doing this? Why was he pushing this topic?*

Sasha could feel her cheeks flush.

"Am I getting too personal?"

"Yes."

"Sorry."

"Yes, American men are different from Russian men." A faint smile curved her lips. *And some are very different from all others.*

Again they moved up in line. It was almost her turn at the check-in.

"Will you go back home after Seattle?" Tru asked.

Sasha nodded.

"You should see a little of the country before you return."

"I have my work. And—" she paused "—other matters to settle."

She was next to check in. Tru figured it was time to go. "Listen," he said awkwardly, "be . . . careful. Don't go playing cops and robbers out there in Seattle now. Leave that to the real cops and robbers. If you do run into any problems, you can always call . . . Del Monte. I've put him on retainer. Any difficulties and he'll fly right out to Seattle and . . . take care of things."

She nodded formally, then switched her satchel to her left hand, extending her right to him. *So, this is it,* she thought, telling herself it was for the best. There truly was something about American men. Or certain American men, anyway. Something all too tantalizing, mesmerizing, dangerous. She fully believed she would feel less threatened and more in control confronting a den of unscrupulous smugglers than spending much time with Truman Fortune.

For a moment, Tru merely looked at Sasha's outstretched hand. Then finally, he took it in his, but instead of a brief, formal shake, he held her hand, moving his thumb lightly over her smooth palm. Their eyes met for an instant, but the moment was too intense and too uncomfortable. Both looked away. The gentleman in front of Sasha stepped back from the counter and it was Sasha's turn to purchase her ticket. There was one problem: Tru hadn't let go of her hand and in fact was gripping it more tightly.

"Please, Tru. I must pay for my ticket."

Then, to her utter surprise, he abruptly turned to the young man behind the counter and asked for two tickets to Seattle.

"Tru...this is not...necessary," she stammered as he hurriedly signed the credit-card slip and took hold of the two tickets. Then he clasped her arm, hurrying her along.

"I do not understand," she protested, baffled by his tense manner.

"Just keep walking and don't look around," he muttered as they wove through the crowds.

Reflexively, she did just as he told her not to do and started to look back. Tru gave her arm a sharp tug.

"All right. All right. But tell me what I am not supposed to see," she demanded as he dragged her in the direction of the boarding gates.

"Our silent pal from the bar."

Sasha stopped short.

"Keep walking," Tru ordered, propelling her forward, his grip on her arm like a vise. "Maybe we can lose him."

"If he does not already know where we are going," she said.

He risked a quick glance behind them.

"Do you see him?"

"No."

But they both realized the rather bland, average-looking man could virtually melt into the crowds, undetected.

Tru checked his watch. "We don't board for ten minutes. If we hang around by the gate, waiting, he's bound to spot us."

"Then, what—?" Before she could finish her question, she found herself being suddenly propelled to the right, down a narrow passageway where Tru had spotted an open door.

"Hurry," he said, pushing her inside the door and skipping in after her, only then realizing their hideout was a large, foul-smelling janitor's closet. He left the door cracked open, partly to keep a watch, partly to dilute the pungent odor of ammonia.

"Please, Tru," she said in a low voice. "My arm."

With a start, he released her. She rubbed the spot.

"I'm sorry. Did I hurt you?"

She shook her head no.

"We'll wait here until it's time to board and then make a run for it."

She nodded.

"Are you okay?"

"You should not do this, Tru. You should not be involved—"

"That's an American man for you," he said with a half smile. "We just can't resist a damsel in distress."

"Believe me, I am most capable of looking after myself," she argued in her typical stoic fashion. "I have never needed to have a man—"

"Never?"

Sasha narrowed her gaze at him.

He grinned. "Okay, so you're not exactly the typical damsel in distress. You're tough, nervy, strong-willed, and you could probably bring most men to their knees with just one of your hard-edged looks."

"So, why are you here?" she asked in her somber, smoky voice that echoed faintly in the tight confines of the closet.

"I guess," he said softly, his hands finding their way to her face, "because my life's been pretty dull and quiet lately, and when it comes right down to it, I like living on the edge. Just like you." He leaned forward to kiss her.

She received his kiss with far more ardor than she intended. Perhaps the ammonia was going to her head, making it hard for her to think straight. Perhaps it was the tension she felt, knowing that the beer drinking man from the bar was out there in the terminal searching for her. Or perhaps she really was a hopeless romantic—no matter how hard she tried to fight it.

"Yes," she confessed weakly, "it is true. I, too, like living on the edge."

His hand moved in a caressing gesture against her cheek. "If we start agreeing all the time, we'll really be in trouble."

THE COAST LOOKED CLEAR as they made a run for their plane. They were the last ones to board. The stewardess, a pert brunette with a winning smile, gave Tru a curious look after a quick survey of his dour, badly dressed companion. Tru and Sasha knew what she was thinking, but they both presented her with blank looks.

The stewardess checked their tickets and directed them to the first-class compartment, which was to their left. Before heading for their section, they nervously glanced down the aisles to the right, surveying the economy-class passengers. After giving each other quick, reassuring looks, they started for their seats.

They were almost there when Sasha took in a harsh breath. Tru saw her gesture almost imperceptibly to her right.

It was the burly man in what looked to be the same cheap black suit, sitting in a first-class window seat, idly reading a magazine. If he was aware of their presence at all, he gave no hint of it. He seemed completely absorbed in what he was reading.

Tru gripped Sasha's arm and hurried her forward into their seats.

"He knows I am going to the funeral," Sasha muttered. "Who is he, do you think? A friend of Drew's? How did he find me in the first place?"

"If he's Russian, he could have followed you from Moscow. Are you sure you never saw him—"

"Not before yesterday. But it is possible I just did not notice him until then."

Tru could feel the adrenaline pumping through him. He glanced over at Sasha. She appeared remarkably composed under the circumstances, but he remembered his own adage—You Can't Tell A Book By Its Cover.

He reached for her hand and gave it a reassuring squeeze. She stared out the window. "If he followed me from Moscow, he could either have been Drew's accomplice or—"

"If he first started following you in Denver, then someone who knew about you put him on to you."

"How could anyone know?"

"Did you tell anyone back in Moscow that you were coming to Denver?"

"Only my superior at work."

"Only?" Tru retorted sardonically.

"I did not think, at the time, there would be a danger in telling him. I said simply that I was going to visit an old friend of the family. Nothing about Drew."

"Did he know you and Drew were married?"

"Well, yes, but—"

"And that he skipped out on you?"

"No. He believes—I told everyone that Drew returned to Chicago for business and that he would be gone for . . . a while. I made no mention, to anyone, that he'd deceived me."

Tru leaned a little closer. "Did you tell anyone—anyone at all—about the icon?"

Sasha looked incredulous. "You think I am an idiot? No. I could trust no one with that information. If anyone else knows about this, it is not from me, but Drew."

Tru nodded slowly. "Okay, we'll just play it cool and I'll try to get a handle on our tail."

Sasha narrowed her gaze. "Please translate."

But Tru wasn't paying attention. He was leaning over into the aisle, pretending to look for something he'd supposedly dropped. Meanwhile he risked a quick glance back.

Sasha gave him a nudge. "It is possible that this is coincidence."

Tru straightened up, responding to her comment with a wry smile.

She shrugged. "But probably not," she conceded, showing remarkable calm. Inwardly, though, her heart was thumping wildly and she found it hard to breathe.

"Do you have a mirror?" Tru asked abruptly.

Sasha was baffled by his request, but she fished in her purse for one.

Tru used it to get a better look at Black Suit.

"What is he doing?"

"Still reading." He palmed the small mirror as a stewardess came by to remind them to snap on their seat belts for takeoff.

A few minutes after they were in flight, Tru again checked out Black Suit in the mirror.

Sasha saw Tru start to rise. She gripped his arm. "Where are you going?"

"To powder my nose."

"What?"

"To the men's room."

"You are sure you will not try to powder his nose?" she asked in a hushed voice, still maintaining her hold on his sleeve.

Tru smiled shyly. "That's an idea."

"Not a good one," she argued, but released her grip so he could leave.

Nervously she glanced back, only to see that the seat occupied by the man who was apparently following her was now empty.

Tru stood waiting outside the door of the toilet cubicle. Above the door, the sign marked Occupied was lit. A moment later the light went off and the door slid open. Sasha wasn't surprised to see who exited. She held her breath as once again she observed Tru say something to the now familiar-looking man. And this time, the man responded briefly, his expression bland, before moving around Tru and returning to his seat. Sasha quickly faced forward, her hand pressed to her chest. She could feel her heart racing.

It seemed like an eternity before Tru sat down beside her again.

"Yes?" she asked.

Tru looked over at her. "He's got an accent. I can't tell for sure if it's Russian, but . . ."

The muscles in Sasha's face constricted. "But it is likely."

He started to reach for her hand, but she turned abruptly to him. "You must not continue with me, Tru. I do not want to be responsible—"

"Whoa. Hold it right there, sugar. No one's been responsible for me for a long time now."

"Why do you do this? You do not know me. You do not have any obligation—"

"I told you. I'm just a guy who digs action and adventure," he said flippantly.

"This is not a joke, Tru."

"I'm not laughing."

"Yes, but you do not understand. It is too dangerous for you to be involved with me. And I . . . do not want . . . to be involved with you. It is not wise. For either of us. It can go nowhere."

Tru studied her. Maybe this was the time to tell Sasha about the tontine. At least then, she wouldn't have to worry that she might once again wind up foolishly and impulsively walking down the aisle with yet another American charmer she hardly knew.

5

AFTER TRU WENT THROUGH a brief rundown of the tontine, Sasha could hardly contain her curiosity. "Why was your father so against marriage?"

Tru smiled wryly. "Let's say he didn't have a great track record and he wanted to save his sons from repeating his mistakes."

"Not a great track record? What does that mean?"

"It means four marriages, four divorces, and a lot of alimony payments," Tru said acerbically. "Dad had a weakness for women that inevitably led to a trip down the aisle."

"And none of these marriages made him . . . happy?"

"For a brief time, I imagine they all did."

"He was happy with your mother for only a brief time, too?" Sasha asked, interested to learn more about Tru's background and relieved to have something other than the stranger in the black suit to think about.

Tru smiled wistfully. "A very brief time. My mother was a photojournalist for an international newsmagazine. The story is, she met my father between a jaunt to Burma and an assignment in Nigeria." His smile turned teasing as he eyed Sasha. "Believe it or not, their whirlwind courtship was even shorter than yours and Cheeseman's. They were married ten days after they met. You could call it a whim on both their parts."

"And then she went to Nigeria?"

"Nigeria, then the Camaroons, Nepal." Tru shrugged. "Supposedly, she realized she was pregnant sometime during a series of interviews with the Dalai Lama. And she always delighted in telling the story of how she delivered me in a rice paddy in Southeast China."

"Your mother sounds . . . remarkable."

"She *was* remarkable." A shadow fell across his features. "She died about ten years ago. Her plane went down over San Salvador."

Sasha instinctively placed her hand over Tru's. "I am so sorry."

Tru smiled nostalgically. "She was a dazzling woman. A firm believer in the individual spirit, outspoken, rebellious. And impossibly reckless."

Sasha's hand remained on Tru's. "You are your mother's child, yes?"

"Maybe more than I even realized."

Sasha felt her pulse quicken. She hastily removed her hand. "So this . . . tontine . . . Perhaps it is a very good thing."

A bead of sweat broke out across Tru's brow as he pretended sudden interest in the complimentary airline magazine protruding from the back pocket of the seat in front of him. "Yes, a very good thing."

"And yet, for two of your brothers, the tontine was not a deterrent. Mr. Del Monte made mention that your brother Adam and your brother Peter have both gotten married."

Tru grew uncomfortable and distractedly plucked out the magazine. "Yes. Yes, that's true. But there were . . . extenuating circumstances."

Sasha smiled faintly. "But you are not worried about . . . extenuating circumstances."

"No. You see, it was different for Adam and Pete."

"Different?"

Tru had hoped she wouldn't pursue it. He should have known better. "Yes. Well . . . neither of them had ever taken many risks before. Adam was always this laid-back playboy, never really taking life seriously. And Pete . . . Pete took life way too seriously. Two extremes. See?"

Sasha thought about it. "I am not sure what it is I am to see."

"What I mean is, both of them were caught off guard. They were . . . unprepared. What happened, really, was that they shifted positions. Adam met Eve and suddenly he began to take life seriously for the first time. A little too seriously, if you ask me."

"And your brother Pete?"

"Pete? Well, Pete met Elizabeth and suddenly he decided it was time to have some . . . fun, let his hair down, be more spontaneous."

"A little too spontaneous, in your opinion?"

Tru grinned. "Hey, I can't complain. They're happy enough and I'm—"

"Rich enough?"

Tru's grin faded. "I know you think all wealthy Americans are decadent, materialistic and extravagant. But you're wrong about some of us. I don't care about money for money's sake, or about being part of a privileged class. I care about innovation, change, reforming the system. I want Fortune's to be a trailblazer into the twenty-first century, a model of how corporations can be run efficiently, cooperatively and creatively, without sacrificing individual rights and needs." He stopped abruptly, realizing he was beginning to sound like he was on a soapbox. He shot Sasha a quick look, expecting her to appear cynical.

Instead, her expression was thoughtful. "Our system has produced its problems, I admit, but it is not good—as you say—to go from one extreme to the other."

"Exactly," he muttered. Tru then idly skimmed the magazine while Sasha stared out the window again.

"Sasha," Tru said, closing the magazine after a couple of minutes. "I don't think we should go to the funeral." He leaned closer to her, dropping his voice to a whisper. "What we should do is ditch this guy at the airport and get you on a plane to New York. And then you can arrange a flight back to Moscow. Once you get home, you can always stick the icon someplace where it can be found but not traced back to you, and—"

"That is a crime. And what if other icons have already been smuggled out of my country? Or if other innocent Russian women are being duped at this very moment by other supposed American businessmen? What if Drew was part of a smuggling ring? It is my responsibility—"

"You're not Wonder Woman, Sasha. You can't tackle something like this single-handedly. It's crazy. And what if Black Suit back there is involved? If he sees you nosing around at the funeral, he could put the wrong two-and-two together and tag you as part of the ring."

"I will have to take that chance," she said stubbornly. "Besides, the icon is still in Moscow."

"Yes, but he doesn't know that. What's going to happen to us if he isn't convinced?"

Tru was relieved to see Sasha mull this over. "You are right, Tru. But it is as I said before. You must not place yourself in danger."

"You're missing the point, Sasha."

"It is you who are missing the point, Tru. I cannot let you—"

"No, I can't let you."

"This is not your responsibility."

"I'm going to have to put my foot down, Sasha."

"Must you always argue?"

"I'm not the one arguing."

"You are like all American men."

"And what's that supposed to mean?"

She gave him a disdainful look. "You do not think a woman can manage without you."

"Certainly not one as pigheaded as you. Certainly not a woman who goes waltzing down the aisle with a smuggler."

"I did not waltz. And I did not know he was a smuggler."

"You know what I'm saying."

Sasha raised a brow. "Even more, I know what it is you are thinking."

They were practically nose to nose, conducting their whole argument in whispers. "And what am I thinking?" he challenged.

"You are afraid."

"Afraid? I'm afraid? No. Oh, no. I'm just not crazy." He tapped his temple with his index finger for emphasis. "I may be reckless on occasion, but I don't go blithely waltzing into a den of thieves—"

"Waltzing. Always waltzing," she snickered.

He smiled condescendingly. "Excuse me, comrade. I suppose I should say, marching. That's what you comrades all do, don't you? March to the same drummer. Always in step."

"I may be only a journalist who mostly follows the trends in agriculture and business, but I have a responsibility as a citizen to my country to unearth the perpetrators of crimes against the state. And to make certain my standing and reputation go unblemished."

Tru sighed wearily. "There's obviously no point arguing with you."

Sasha folded her arms across her chest. "That is true."

"If I can't talk any sense into you, I'll just have to take matters into my own hands."

"And what does this mean?"

"It means I'm sticking you on a flight for New York as soon as we land, whether you like it or not. You're getting in over your head here and I'm not going to stand by and watch you drown."

Sasha was indignant. "I am an excellent swimmer. And I've already told you I do not want you to watch. When we land, you must be the one to leave. Return to Denver. Return to your work. I do not need your advice or your help," she concluded with a defiant shake of her head.

"You need it," he muttered, grabbing up his magazine again. "You're just too damn stubborn to take it."

They didn't speak for the rest of the flight.

When they landed, Sasha once again stayed in her seat while the other passengers, including Black Suit, filed out. Sasha imagined he would be waiting for her in the crowd out in the terminal. Her chest tightened and she felt a prickle of fear, but ignored it, determined not to give Tru, who remained sitting beside her, even a hint that she was afraid.

She finally turned to him. "I do not wish to part with bad feelings, Tru. I understand that you mean well, but you do not have to worry about me. I will be cautious. But I cannot turn back now."

Tru gave her a faint nod. Somehow, he felt as if his fate had been signed, sealed and delivered the day Sasha came into his life—that it had all been decided then and there. He didn't like it one bit, but he didn't know how to fight fate.

On impulse, Sasha leaned closer and gave him a chaste peck on the lips. As she drew back, Tru's hand cuffed her neck, pulling her back to him. This time the kiss was anything but chaste. Nor could Sasha define it as passionate. It was nothing like those kisses they'd shared in the cabin last night. No, this kiss was hard-edged with frustration.

SASHA'S TEMPLE BEAT like a drum as she looked nervously about the terminal for Black Suit.

"I don't see him," Tru said.

"Maybe he goes already to the funeral, knowing I will be there."

"I don't think so. He'll want to keep an eye on you from here on out, so he can see if you hand the goods over to someone."

"Then he will be disappointed." She turned to Tru, extending her hand. "We shall say goodbye here, yes?"

He grabbed her hand and started pulling her toward the exit doors. "We shall say goodbye here, no?" he retorted angrily.

She tugged against him. "I thought it was understood—"

"Can't you stop arguing with me for one minute?"

"I am not the one who is arguing." She struggled to free herself from his grasp, but Tru's hold was like steel.

"You're not only arguing," he hissed, "you're making a scene!"

"Oh, you are insufferable!"

Tru grinned. "Flattery will get you anywhere, comrade."

SASHA STOWED HER satchel in a locker and they caught a cab outside the terminal. It was a little past two o'clock, but the airport wasn't far from the city and the driver assured them they'd make the funeral on time.

As they rode into Seattle, Sasha was momentarily distracted by the spectacular vista of evergreen-covered hills and water, water, everywhere. And, as if to welcome the newcomer to the sparkling emerald city, the Seattle sky was clear blue without a cloud in sight.

"What is that?" Sasha asked, pointing in the distance to a structure that resembled a flying saucer on top of a six-hundred-foot tripod.

"The Space Needle," Tru and the cabbie said in unison. "What the Eiffel Tower is to Paris, the Space Needle is to Seattle," Tru went on to explain. He glanced over at her. "Say the word and we can skip the funeral and go sight-seeing instead. There's a spectacular view—"

"I am not here for sight-seeing," she said in her most officious voice, partly to conceal her mounting nervousness.

THE CHAPEL WHERE Martin Baker's funeral was being held was in a downtown section of the city, close to Elliott Bay. Sasha and Tru arrived about ten minutes early. Tru took Sasha's arm as they stepped inside the small, cool chapel. There were about two dozen people inside, mostly men, most of them wearing conservative blue or black suits. Sasha knew her imagination was probably getting the upper hand, but they all looked rather sinister to her. Tru gestured toward a back pew, but she headed up the aisle to where the open casket was on display. She really had no doubt in her mind that Martin Baker was Drew Cheeseman, but she felt compelled to make sure.

Tru was right behind her as she regarded the handsome body peacefully laid out in a tailored blue suit. Yes, it was Drew. Her husband. Her deceiver. Her knees went weak and she swayed against Tru, grateful for his supportive arm around her waist. Her eyes closed for a moment and she felt her first real sense of sorrow and loss. In spite of his deception, there had been moments between them....

"Are you okay?" Tru's voice was tender with concern.

Sasha nodded, opening her eyes. As they turned around, Tru with his arm still around her waist, she looked with curiosity at the very attractive young brunette sitting in the front pew. She held a hankie clutched in one palm as she dabbed at her eyes. A handsome dark-haired man in a well-tailored blue suit, who looked to be in his mid-thirties, was comforting her. There was something vaguely familiar about this man.

When Tru squeezed her waist, Sasha was diverted from her scrutiny of the couple in the front pew by the arrival of the familiar black-suited man who was quietly slipping into an empty back row. Sasha had known he'd be here, but still his presence made her tremble. She felt Tru's grip tighten reassuringly around her waist. This time she gave him a grateful smile.

There was space in the pew behind the pretty brunette and her comforting friend. Sasha moved in and sat down, with Tru taking the aisle seat beside her. He, too, was curious about the pair. Grieving siblings? he wondered.

Sasha leaned forward a little, trying to get a better view of the man who looked so familiar. And then it hit her. Yes. That first day at the convention—her first meeting with Drew. It had been like in all the American romance movies. She and Drew had glanced at each other across a crowded room and their glances held. And then, as if in slow motion, he'd started making his way toward her. Sasha remembered how her heart had raced, how she'd followed his approach as though he were the only person in the room. She also remembered, with great embarrassment, how she even heard violins playing. . . . But now she remembered something else. Before Drew started toward her, he'd been talking to another man, a colleague who also sold farm machinery. The man sitting in the front pew comforting the brunette was that man. Sasha was certain of it. So he, too, knew *Drew Cheeseman.*

As the organ started to play, Sasha leaned very close to Tru and whispered her discovery to him. Tru took this news with a mixture of excitement and alarm. The excitement was pure instinct. The alarm was something else. A part of him had hoped Sasha would learn nothing at the funeral and he'd be able to get her out of there without incident and on a plane bound for Moscow before any further complications ensued. Tru was honest enough to admit to himself that he wasn't only thinking of their physical welfare, but their emotional welfare, too.

The organ stopped, and a minister stepped up to the pulpit. The mourners all rose. Tru quickly glanced back at Black Suit and was startled to see that he was no longer alone in the pew. Indeed, he was now flanked on either side by men in blue suits. And Black Suit didn't look pleased. This was getting "curiouser and curiouser."

The minister was finishing a brief prayer. There was a low murmur of "Amens" and everyone sat down—everyone except the attractive dark-haired man in the front pew, who now came up to the pulpit. As he took his place, his eyes scanned the group gathered to pay their last respects to travel agent, Martin Baker—or smuggler, Drew Cheeseman, as it were. Sasha's breath caught as his gaze came to rest for a moment on her. Was that a smile she saw or just the way the light struck his face? If it was a smile, there was nothing warm or friendly about it.

Meanwhile Tru focused his attention on Black Suit, who was still sandwiched in between the Blue Suits. Black Suit looked none too happy with his companions. Tru watched him smooth his hair back in a nervous gesture and whisper something to the short, thickset Blue Suit on his right. The man made no response. Black Suit started to rise, but the Blue Suit on his left—a taller version of the man on his right—shot him a look. If looks could kill, Tru thought, a chill zigzagging down his spine. Black Suit settled back into his seat. For a moment, his eyes locked with Tru's. Now it was Tru's turn to get one of those looks!

"...to say that Martin Baker was a friend always ready to lend a helping hand, always there in times of need, generous to a fault, as honest as the day is long..."

Sasha nudged Tru.

"...sad to know that he leaves not only his friends, but his grieving widow, who would like to say a few parting words...."

Sasha had a few parting words to say, all right, but she certainly never dreamed she'd be acknowledged and called upon to give them.

Only *she* wasn't being called upon, after all. While Sasha was getting over the shock, the brunette from the front pew was making her way up to the pulpit.

Tru turned to Sasha. She turned to him. Flies could have flown into both their mouths!

"At least we had three wonderful years together," the brunette was saying.

Sasha took in her words in stunned silence. Three years. Then, not only was her marriage to Drew Cheeseman the worst mistake of her life; it wasn't even a legitimate marriage. Actually, once she absorbed the shock of this discovery, she felt a little better. So, she never was married to Drew in truth. She was not a widow—and certainly now, not a *grieving* widow.

Sasha sensed Tru's concern, and gave him a whisper of a smile.

There was a brief reception in one of the basement rooms of the chapel after the funeral. Tru didn't even waste his breath trying to talk Sasha out of attending. As he escorted her downstairs, he saw that each of the mourners was waiting in line to offer condolences to the widow. Sasha didn't join the line immediately, but headed instead for the attractive dark-haired man who'd spoken the eulogy. Tru was right on her heels, determined to keep a close watch on her.

"You gave a moving speech," she began pleasantly.

"Thank you." The man showed no sign of recognition. Nor any sign of curiosity.

"Martin Baker must have been a very close friend of yours?" Sasha said.

"Yes."

Tru reached out his hand toward the man. "Jack Fisher. I met your friend in Chicago a few months back. Nice guy. I didn't catch your name."

"Bill Hovy."

"Jack Fisher" shook Hovy's hand. While the man might have looked as cool as a cucumber, Tru noticed that the hand he shook was clammy as all get-out. Tru put an arm around Sasha's shoulder. "And I suppose you know Anna. Anna . . . Christie."

Sasha could barely contain her urge to grin. *Why not Anna Karenina!*

Bill Hovy nodded noncommittally, then looked over at the grieving widow. "Well, if you'll excuse me, I should lend some moral support to Deidre."

"Ah, yes," Sasha replied. "We, too must pay our respects to poor Deidre. To think. Three blissful years of marriage. And then, one day, her husband steps out the door. She expects him back anytime. She waits. She begins to grow anxious when he does not reappear. What thoughts must have gone through her mind...?"

Sasha and Tru both saw the muscles constrict in Hovy's face. "I really must . . . Excuse me. . . ."

"Of course," Sasha responded with exaggerated sympathy.

"I was just wondering, Bill. Did they catch the mugger?" Tru asked in a low voice just as Hovy was almost out of earshot.

Hovy turned around, his nicely tanned face losing a bit of color. "No. No, they haven't yet."

SASHA AND TRU SLIPPED out of the chapel, both of them surveying the street. Neither Black Suit nor his two companions were anywhere in the vicinity.

"Are you okay?" Tru asked.

"There is so much I must follow up on. Did you see how nervous this Hovy was? And the grieving widow, Deidre. The whole time we were talking to Hovy, I could feel her watching us. And when I paid my regrets and took her hand for a moment, it was trembling badly."

"You'd be trembling, too, if your husband just—" Tru stopped, smiling crookedly. "Sorry. I never did win any awards for tact."

Sasha smiled back. "He was not my husband, it seems."

"No. I guess you're right."

"Come. Let us get something to eat and make our plans. There is a restaurant just across the street."

"Sasha."

"There is much to go on now, Tru. I must talk again with this Hovy."

"Talk about what?" Tru asked cautiously.

Sasha raised an eyebrow. "Ah, reminisce about Moscow, perhaps. Discuss farm machinery...and other items of interest."

"Sasha, if Hovy was there with Cheeseman—"

"Oh, I am certain of it, Tru. I am certain he can tell me a great deal. You saw how nervous he was."

"Maybe he can tell you a lot. The question is—why would he? Especially if it means incriminating himself?" Tru argued.

Sasha started across the street, with Tru by her side. "The answer is simple. He very likely wants the icon. And I have it."

Tru grabbed Sasha's arm as they got to the island in the middle of the wide street. "You're playing with fire here and you're likely to be the one who ends up getting burned," he began to protest.

"And Deidre, too," Sasha mused, ignoring Tru's warning. "Oh, yes. She may have been married to Martin Baker, but she knows something of Drew Cheeseman. I feel certain of it. I must meet with each of them, play them one against the other—"

"Sasha . . ."

But she was already stepping out off the curb. Again, Tru made a grab for her. Only this time it wasn't to argue with her, but to keep her from getting run over by a blue sedan that was barreling toward them.

At first, when the car screeched to a stop, Tru assumed the driver was merely upset and wanted to mouth off at Sasha for not watching where she was going. Too late, he recognized the short, thickset man behind the wheel.

The back door was slung open as the driver's tall companion prepared to step out. Sasha gasped as she saw a gun in his hand. He motioned with the gun for them to get in.

Tru, noting that Black Suit wasn't along for the ride, gripped Sasha's hand, holding her back. Surely the gunman wouldn't shoot them in broad daylight with pedestrians and other vehicles coming and going on the street. He went to pull Sasha away from the car, forcing their assailant to either make himself and his gun more visible—which Tru doubted he would do—or give up—at least for now—and take off. But before he knew what was happening, Sasha wrenched her hand free. To his amazement Tru saw her leg shoot out against the open rear door, and the man with the gun was groaning in pain as the door slammed into him.

"Hurry," she hissed, grabbing Tru's hand as they darted around the car and across the street.

They continued running along the sidewalk, not even looking back this time, for fear it would slow them down. Their only thought was escape.

"Here!" Tru shouted, having regrouped a bit. He pushed her ahead of him into a laundromat, figuring there'd be a rear exit to a parking area. Which there was.

The lot led to a narrow deserted street. Tru dared a glance over his shoulder. He spotted the shorter of the two men at the back door of the laundromat. Grabbing Sasha, he pressed her into the rear entrance of a four-storey apartment building.

"Are they—?" she started to ask breathlessly.

Tru nodded, placing one hand over her mouth to silence her, reaching for the doorknob with the other. *No give. Damn.* It was locked. A cold sweat was punctuating his forehead. Sasha, too, tried the door.

They could hear footsteps now. Cautious. Menacing.

There was no place to hide. Any moment now, they would be discovered hovering in the doorway. Tru's hands clenched into fists. He hadn't gotten into a knockdown, no-holds-barred fight in years. Hell, he was overdue.

But just as the footsteps grew closer and Tru was preparing to do battle, shoving Sasha protectively behind him, the door to the apartment house fell open as a haggard-looking middle-aged woman was exiting, carrying a plastic bin loaded with laundry. She gave the pair a bland, disinterested look as they slipped inside.

Their luck continued to hold. Just as they burst out the front door of the apartment building, they saw a crowded trolley car about to pull out from the curb.

They raced for it and climbed on, pushing in among other passengers as it began to move.

Tru and Sasha were both sweating profusely and out of breath.

"That was a close call," Tru murmured, as the jerking motion of the trolley pressed him up against Sasha. He held on to a pole, snaking his free hand around her waist—to help her keep her balance, he lied to himself.

Sasha leaned into him. "Very close," she said in breathless little gasps.

Tru knew she was as aroused and exhilarated by the chaos and danger as he was.

Suddenly the trolley jerked to a stop. Tru was still holding her close—too close for comfort.

"There's a hotel," she said, pointing across the way. Tru loosened his grip on her and followed her off the trolley.

The Danford Hotel had an oddly tropical feel, with its potted palms and oversize wicker furniture dotting the spacious lobby. The sea-green carpeting added to the effect. After Tru registered—as Mr. and Mrs. Parks from Omaha, Nebraska—and explained that they had no luggage because of a mix-up at the airport, he hurriedly steered Sasha toward the elevator.

The doors shut and they were alone. "You might have mentioned you knew karate."

She smiled, her cheeks flushed, her hair in disarray. "I told you I was well able to take care of myself, yes?"

"Do all Russian women know self-defense?" he asked suspiciously.

A faint smile played on Sasha's lips. "I learn from friend who is instructor in the martial arts."

"A good friend?"

"Yes." Her smile deepened. "She is very good friend. Like sister."

THE HOTEL SUITE, like the lobby, was outfitted with green carpeting and wicker furnishings. Colorful art posters decorated the walls. There was a small sitting room and one bedroom with a queen-size bed.

Tru phoned Jessica, just to tell her he'd decided to accompany Sasha to Seattle after all. After surveying the bedroom, Sasha looked questioningly over at Tru as he hung up. Tru peeked into the room and saw what was troubling her.

Smiling wryly, he pointed to a small couch in the sitting room. "A lot better than two wooden chairs."

"But not nearly so funny," she said in that smoky voice of hers.

He took in a deep breath. Even the sound of his breathing was erotic to her. A ribbon of warmth spread through her body. She told herself to stop it. How could she want him again so badly? It had only been last night.... But her body didn't seem concerned about decent intervals. Perhaps it was all relative. Perhaps she was obsessed with him.

Tru was having his own struggles. Last night in the cabin, it had been lust, pure and simple, he told himself. And it had been the same for Sasha. He considered the circumstances, the rainstorm, the one bed, Sasha, all damp and rosy from the shower.... Okay, they'd both succumbed to yearnings. But the yearning he felt now was different, more diffuse, far more worrisome. He cared about her. She moved him like no other woman. He was scared. And he had every reason to be scared.

He smiled crookedly. "We could both use a few laughs right about now," he quipped, trying for some levity.

Sasha smiled back, but it was nervousness not amusement. "Perhaps you know a good joke...." She, too, tried for a light note. But even as she fought against the urge, she moved slowly toward him.

Tru nodded. "Right. A good joke..." But nothing the least bit funny was entering his head.

She was standing before him now. "Make me laugh again, Tru," she whispered throatily.

As if by its own will, his hand moved to her hair, freeing it from its pins. Her wheat-colored locks fell around her shoulders in careless, lustrous waves.

"Oh, Tru, I keep thinking.... I cannot help myself. I cannot stop thinking...." Passion, recklessly ignited, had already put her in serious jeopardy. "This is not smart...."

Fierce, electric attraction mingled with nervous tension. "If we were smart, we'd quit playing detective and clear out of town." Tru attempted to sound resolute. He tried even harder to keep his fingers out of her hair. He struck out on both counts.

"If we were so smart, Tru, would we be here together now, like this?" An aching need enveloped her. Her hands, almost as if they weren't her own, crept up his chest, across his shoulders, around his neck.

"This is ... risky, Sasha." The risks were escalating by the heartbeat.

"But we are attracted to risk, yes?" She searched his face for confirmation.

He pulled her close, all remnants of caution dissolving, the desire he'd held in check since that morning evaporating in one breath. "Yes. Oh, yes, yes, Sasha. Yes..."

With an urgency and abandon that stunned them both, Sasha tore at his clothes. Astonished but inspired by her lack of inhibition, Tru followed suit, ripping at the buttons of her blouse. His hands were shaking, his dexterity was at an all-time low. Sasha helped him. He took great pleasure in tossing her dreadful brown outfit aside. He took greater pleasure, still, in ridding her of her utilitarian undergarments. But the greatest pleasure of all awaited him: The sight of Sasha's exquisite body took his breath away. Last night he'd possessed her in darkness, now he would make love to her in the light. Her skin was creamy white, flawless. He let his hands glide down over her throat, her high, voluptuous breasts. He caressed her flat stomach, feeling her muscles constrict. He growled with pleasure.

Sasha, surveying his naked body with equal delight, growled back. And then, arms encircling each other, they sank down onto the carpet, laughing softly....

6

"OKAY, SO THIS REAL braggart of a Texan is in this cab in Paris, see. The cabbie's showing him the sights."

Sasha stretched languorously against Tru, her fingers skimming down his bare chest. "Yes. The sights. Lovely sights."

Tru grinned. "Thanks. I mean, right. So the Texan points to this building and he asks the cabbie, 'What's that place?' And the cabbie very proudly says, 'Notre Dame, *monsieur.*'"

Sasha's lips cruised his neck. His skin gave off a warm, fragrant tang.

Tru angled his head to give her more room. "Mmm, that's nice."

"Go on," she prompted.

"Where . . . was I?"

"Notre Dame," she whispered breathily against his ear.

His hands moved down her body in long, lush strokes. "It really isn't all that funny."

"You must not stop."

"I won't," he murmured, planting a row of kisses from her throat to her breast.

She moaned softly and cupped his face, lifting it. "No, I mean the joke, you foolish man. I must hear the punch line."

"I have a much better way to put a smile on your face."

"First the joke, comrade."

He sighed, but rolled over onto his back, cradling his arms behind his head. "Okay. But you're not going to find it funny."

"Go ahead. Notre Dame, *monsieur*."

He gave her a crooked smile. "Right. So the Texan drawls, 'Hell, sonny, back in Texas we could put up a building like that in a couple of weeks.'"

Sasha grinned. "That is funny."

"That's not the punch line."

"Oh," Sasha said contritely. "Sorry. Go ahead."

He started to roll over toward her, but Sasha stopped him midroll. He rolled back. "So a little later they pass another sight. And the Texan asks—"

"'What is that?'"

"Very good. And the cabbie very proudly says—"

"'The Eiffel Tower, *monsieur*.'"

"Say, have you heard this joke before?" he asked bemused.

She smiled brightly. "Never."

"Okay, so the Texan drawls—"

"'Back in Texas we can put up one of those towers in a week.'" Sasha did her best to imitate a Texan drawl. Combined with the Russian accent, it was a lot funnier than the joke.

Tru laughed, pinching her bottom playfully. "Who's telling this joke, anyway?"

"I give the punch line?" she asked innocently.

"No, you do not give the punch line," he replied, imitating her accent now, which made Sasha giggle. She pressed against him, her hand on his thigh.

"This is a very long joke, yes? Are all American jokes so long?"

He cocked his head toward her. "It's a short joke. You just keep interrupting."

She went to pull her hand away, but he clamped his hand over hers. "I'm not complaining."

"So, this Texan . . . What happens next?"

"You're not going to laugh."

Her hand began a slow, sensual slide up his thigh. "Tell me."

"Okay, my persuasive comrade, you win. So, they're driving awhile and the cabbie's passing the Louvre. And the Texan drawls—"

"'What's that building?'"

Tru nodded, pressing a finger against her lips. "And the cabbie gives the Texan a very Parisian shrug and says, '*Je ne sais pas, monsieur.* It wasn't here this morning!'"

"That's it," he said, disappointed by Sasha's blank response. "That's the punch line. It wasn't here this morning." He shook his head. "See, I told you. . . ."

"It wasn't here this morning," Sasha repeated slowly, contemplatively.

"Not funny, right? Dumb. I told you. . . ."

"Terrible," Sasha murmured, pressing her face into Tru's chest. "It wasn't here this morning." And then, suddenly, she burst into laughter. "That is—the worst—joke," she gasped, laughing so hard now, she couldn't catch her breath.

Tru started laughing because she was laughing, but he was utterly puzzled by her response. "So, why—are you—laughing?"

She tried to speak over her giggles. "I think—because—your French accent is—so—funny, *monsieur.* And the joke—is so—foolish."

Still laughing with Sasha, Tru rolled her over, moving on top of her. "By Jove, she's got it. I think she's got it," he said in a bad imitation of Professor Higgins from *My Fair Lady.*

Their laughter faded as she arched against him. Tru closed his eyes, sliding his hands over the luscious perfection of her full breasts, her narrow waist, her wonderfully curved hips, her long, creamy legs. He drew a breath, savoring the milky softness of her skin, still incredulous that this playful, adventurous, uninhibited beauty had emerged as if from a chrysalis from the humorless, hard-nosed ideologue he'd first encountered. Was it only the danger that had infused their last two days together which had caused this transformation? Not only in Sasha, he realized, but in himself, as well. He'd never felt quite this way before. The rough edges of his personality had softened. In the past he had always been tough, objective, even callous toward women. He was a hell-raiser, hell-bent on his freedom; and wary whenever he felt that freedom threatened. But now he suddenly felt more open, more vulnerable—feelings he'd always guarded against—and yet that didn't seem to bother him.

He was hot, burning. *No*, he thought with a start, it wasn't only the danger—at least not for him. It was Sasha herself. He was irresistibly drawn to her "impossible" qualities as well as her enchanting attributes. Making love with her was different from making love with any other woman. There was a special intimacy, and the danger and excitement only made him feel the bond between them more intensely. The true danger here, he realized, was not from the threatening forces outside these four walls, but from the ones within.

Sasha felt Tru tense and she softly kissed his lips. "It is all right," she told him. "You are safe, comrade."

He propped himself on his elbows over her. "Safe? You're . . . on the Pill, then?"

Smiling, she smoothed back his thick, dark hair. "Yes, that, too. But I mean...we can make love without waltzing, yes?"

At first he didn't get it. *Waltzing?* But then he remembered his snide remark on the plane about how she'd gone waltzing down the aisle on the arm of a smuggler.

She drew him down to her, Tru offering no resistance. "I am lousy dancer," she whispered, sliding her tongue provocatively down the side of his neck, her hand sinuously stroking his buttocks.

Tru lowered his mouth to her breast, inscribing a tiny circle around her taut nipple, making her laugh; a different type of laugh this time—sultry, seductive, earthy. He sought her lips. "But a terrific lover..." He breathed the words into her mouth.

Sasha inhaled sharply, as if to swallow his words, swallow a part of him. The very rhythm of his words was erotic. It was all happening again—the wild desire, the reckless abandon, the explosive yearning. She had experienced some of this with her husband, but there was a new dimension with Tru that transcended the purely physical need she had felt with Drew—the raw desire that made it so easy for him to get exactly what he wanted: a wife, a stooge. She hadn't been able to resist Drew's sexual magnetism; it had overwhelmed her. The physical bond had made everything else seem unimportant at the time. She'd asked him so little, accepted whatever he'd told her. And he'd seemed only to care that she wanted him, couldn't resist him. There had been no curiosity, no interest, no real communication between them. With Drew, it had only been her body that spoke.

And that was the heart of the difference. With Tru, her body sang. Tru made her laugh. Tru infuriated her. Tru entranced her. Tru frustrated her. Her emotions were in constant turmoil. Oh, what was to become of her?

But then Tru's mouth was at her throat, one hand moving sinuously along her inner thigh, the other caressing her breast, sculpting it with his fingers. Her heart raced, her hips moved against him, seeking, wanting. She made a small sound deep in her throat, a cat's purr. And again her body sang as he entered her—a divine aria this time....

TRU ROLLED OVER, reaching out for her instinctively. The bed was empty. His eyes shot open and he sprang up.

"Sasha?"

A sigh of relief escaped his lips as she stepped out of the bathroom, but he was admittedly disappointed to see that she was already fully dressed—his dour proletariat once more.

"Is it morning already, comrade?" he asked teasingly. But his expression reflected a shadow of concern. He didn't want her to say again that they must forget the passion they'd shared. He was long past being able to forget. And he believed she was, too. Or at least he hoped she was.

"It is well after my usual time of rising," she replied stiffly as she watched him throw off the covers, get out of bed and walk toward her. She tried to ignore that he was naked and so at ease about it. But such a splendid body was impossible to disregard.

"There is much to do today," she said, stepping back as he approached.

He was at her side, his hands reaching out for her shoulders.

"Please, Tru..."

He rested his forehead against hers. "It's easy to please Tru," he murmured.

Sasha pinched his ass.

He grinned. "That's a start."

"Be serious, Tru. I must go and have a talk with this man from the funeral, Bill Hovy. And then . . . the wife. Deidre."

Tru pulled back, and said incredulously, "You're kidding. Russian humor, right?"

Sasha scowled. "They can give me answers. . . ."

Tru scowled, too. "They can get you killed."

"I will arrange to meet them in an open place where there are many people. . . ."

"What makes you think either of them will come?"

Sasha hesitated. Tru saw two pink spots on her cheeks. His gaze narrowed. "You've already arranged it. You've already spoken to them. While I was sleeping."

Sasha mustered a defiant look. "This is true. This is the purpose of my being here. . . ."

Tru dropped his hands to his sides. "Right. I guess you just got sidetracked for a few hours. That seems to be a weakness of yours."

"Do not be cruel, Tru. It is not like you." Her voice held a faint quiver.

"You weren't even going to wake me, were you? You were going to skip out of here—"

"I knew you would not be happy with the arrangement—"

"Not happy with the arrangement? You bet I'm not happy with the arrangement!"

Sasha wished he were dressed. It was most disconcerting having an argument with a naked man—especially one who filled you with such desire. . . .

"I must go, Tru. I will be fine."

"Sure. Sure, you will. Hey, one of those creeps from the funeral makes a move on you and you can floor them with one of your karate chops. And if that fails—" Suddenly he lunged for her, his hands moving roughly up and down her body.

"What are you doing?"

"What? No piece?" Frustration, anger and fear made him keep manhandling her. "Or are you going to pick one up on the way? I bet you shoot straight from the hip. Or, if need be, right in the back. Get 'em when their guard's down, when they're not looking—"

"Please, Tru . . ."

"I'm not pleased, damn it," he snapped, pulling her closer, giving her a hard, bruising kiss.

Sasha let out a little cry, but then her arms encircled his neck and she pressed into his naked body. Their kiss lengthened, no longer angry but filled with wrenching passion. Tru hooked his hands in her hair, and her bobby pins went flying, his bare chest heaving against her.

With her skirt hiked up, he half carried her to the bed. And he kept whispering her name in a voice that seemed to reverberate inside her head.

Sasha welcomed his weight on top of her. She felt his urgency like her own. They climaxed together—without words, without preamble. Quickly the powerful explosions came, and they both lost touch with the world in the sweet rush of orgasm.

It took longer for them to catch their breath. Tru rolled off her, stretching out on the bed. Sasha made no move, even though she felt she must look ridiculous, fully clothed, her skirt like an accordion around her hips, and her panties—somewhere. But she couldn't budge. She felt she must lie very still so that the energy could flow back into her body.

Tru stared up at the ceiling. "What time are you supposed to meet them?"

"Hovy at noon." She had to gather some air into her lungs. "Deidre at one."

"Where?"

"The Space Needle." A smile curved her lips. "Do you know, back in Moscow, we could put up one of those in a day?" She watched his face, hoping to see him smile, too. But no.

"Okay," he said finally. "No more jokes. This is the way it's going to be. No hotdogging."

"Hotdogging? That is what you Americans eat at baseball games, yes?"

"I mean, no going it alone. No sneaking off behind my back. No taking crazy risks. And stop saying, 'I'll be fine.' I don't want you feeling too cocky. I know how dangerous it is to feel too cocky, believe me."

She rolled onto her side, facing him. "Yes?"

His hands found their way to her face. The warmth of her cheeks radiated against his palms. "Just when you're feeling too sure of yourself is when you can be taken by surprise." He gently kissed her bruised lips. "I don't think I'll ever be too sure of myself again, comrade," he murmured. Which, all in all, he thought, was probably a good thing. Otherwise, he might start encouraging Sasha to take dance lessons. It was some small comfort to remember that he was a pretty lousy dancer, himself. And it was tough to teach an old hound new steps!

THEY HAD ALMOST AN HOUR before the meeting with Hovy at the Space Needle and Tru insisted they make a stop at the Fortune's store in downtown Seattle along the way. He was particularly concerned that Sasha's "uniform" and hairstyle made her a sitting duck if either

Black Suit or the pair of Blue Suits were on the lookout for her.

"Is this really necessary, Tru?" Sasha protested as they entered the store. "I have a change of clothing in my satchel at the airport."

"Forget the airport for now. Those creeps might think you're going to bolt, now that they've missed their chance to grab you."

"What I don't understand is that you say you do not think the Russian is working with the two men who almost kidnapped us. The only answer must be that the Russian is a spy and the men in the blue suits are part of Drew's smuggling ring."

Tru was leading her up the escalator to the executive offices where he'd arrange to have one of the buyers make the clothing selections for them so they could remain out of sight. Tru knew he was probably being paranoid, imagining that anyone could have tracked them to the department store, but it was possible he'd been recognized since the Fortune brothers had received a lot of press because of the tontine business, especially with Adam and Pete both tying the knot. Tru had tried to remain in the background, but he hadn't been all that successful. In any case, it didn't hurt to keep a low profile and not take any unnecessary risks.

"I don't know much about spies except from thrillers and movies," Tru commented, "but I wouldn't have thought one of them could be easily intimidated. And Black Suit was sweating bullets when the two Blue Suits sandwiched him in at the church."

"Sweating bullets? I shall remember that one," Sasha mused.

Tru smiled, taking her hand as they stepped off the escalator on the seventh floor. But as they headed down the corridor, past the swing doors marked Executive Personnel Only, his smile faded. "There's always the chance that the Blue Suits are CIA or maybe FBI, and they suspect the Russian is one of Drew's accomplices. And you. Or probably now, both of us."

Sasha appeared downcast. "Oh, Tru . . ."

He put his arm around her. "Not a word. I signed on for the adventure, remember? You did your best to talk me out of it."

"Yes, but . . ." Although she was now trying very hard to keep her escalating emotions in check, her cheeks were flushed. "I must confess, I am . . . glad I did not succeed."

Tru stopped her dead in her tracks and pulled her to him right there in the corridor in front of an open door of one of the VIP offices. "So am I, baby. So am I," he murmured against her lips, then sealed the words with a kiss.

"Excuse me, sir," a man interrupted.

Tru kept hold on Sasha as he turned his head to eyeball the intruder behind him. "Is there a problem?"

"I think you may be in the wrong place. Perhaps a hotel might be more what you have in mind," the middle-aged man in the three-piece suit said bluntly, his expression supercilious. And from his expression, it was evident he didn't quite understand the attraction here.

Tru read the nameplate on his door behind the man. "Dennis Drake, Executive Assistant."

Dennis Drake folded his arms across his chest. "This area is solely for personnel of Fortune's. We have very strict rules—"

"I'm glad to hear it, Denny." Tru winked at Sasha. "Aren't you, comrade?"

"Oh, yes," she said somberly. "Strict rules are most vital."

"I'm afraid I'm going to have to ask the two of you to leave these premises."

Tru gave the man a thumbs-up sign. "Excellent, Den. Direct, polite, just the right touch of authority coupled with a hint of a threat. You are prepared to call in the security guards if we cause a fuss, am I right?"

Dennis was flustered by Tru's insouciance, but he held his ground. "I certainly am, but I truly hope that won't be necessary."

Tru smiled. "Relax, Dennis. It won't be necessary."

"You'll leave quietly?"

Tru's smile deepened. "No. But I'll introduce myself. The name's Truman Fortune. I believe," he said, shifting slightly so that he had a better view inside Drake's office, "that you'll see some similarity between that portrait of my dad you have hanging on your wall and my mug." Tru aped his father's sincere expression.

Dennis Drake was clearly at a loss. If this stranger was pulling his leg, he might have a real nut-case on his hands. On the other hand . . .

Drake did glance back into his office at the portrait and then return to Tru.

"Actually, there really isn't much of a similarity. I more closely resemble my mother," Tru admitted, pulling out his wallet to show the distraught executive assistant his ID.

Drake blanched, but Tru quickly reassured him that he'd handled the situation admirably although he might have been just a shade less haughty. "I guess my sage advice is, Den, never be too sure of yourself," Tru concluded.

A half hour later, the newly attired pair exited Fortune's. Tru, who'd arrived in Seattle in *Rebel Without a Cause* black garb, now looked like your average Joe in a pair of khaki chinos, pin-striped white shirt, and a navy windbreaker. With the help of a little hair spray, he'd even managed to change his hairstyle.

Sasha's transformation was even more extreme, thanks to the buyer, Linda Farrell, who had a real flare for makeovers. Linda had combed Sasha's hair loose, then subdued it with a white headband. A touch of blush and lipstick, just a flick or two of mascara, and Sasha looked like a wholesome young thing who might have been a cheerleader back in high school. The outfit Linda chose for her heightened the image: trim off-white jersey pants—offering more freedom of movement than a skirt in case they had to make another run for it—a muted blue, gray and cream-colored cotton blouse, and an off-white jersey jacket. Sasha looked fresh and smart, and yet would blend into a crowd very nicely. Indeed, Tru and Sasha looked like a pair of young marrieds from someplace like Sacramento or Portland, here in Seattle for a little vacation. Tru even sported a camera. But it wasn't the sights he intended to snap pictures of.

THE SPACE NEEDLE, once the centerpiece of the 1962 World's Fair, had been erected as an example of a future architectural trend that never materialized. This hadn't dampened its popularity over the years, since the Space Needle's real claim to fame were the spectacular 360-degree vistas from its observation tower, aided by high-powered telescopes with nifty zoom lenses.

Tru and Sasha got to the famous structure just as the clock struck noon. They melted into the crowd of tourists at the observation tower, and began to search the faces for Bill Hovy.

"I don't see him," Sasha whispered, not wanting anyone close by to notice her Russian accent.

"Maybe he changed his mind." Tru found the thought comforting. He had no idea what Sasha hoped to gain from this dialogue with Hovy. Surely he wouldn't just blithely incriminate himself. And even if he did, what then? Did Sasha think she could simply turn him over to the authorities? Whatever Hovy might confess to her— no doubt in hopes of getting his hands on the icon—he certainly wasn't going to confess to the police. It would be Sasha's and his word against Hovy's. And if the authorities believed Sasha was involved—

"Look!" Sasha gave him a not-so-delicate nudge in the ribs. "There he is. Getting off the elevator."

Tru grabbed her arm, drawing her away from Hovy's line of sight. "Let's just make sure he's alone first."

They hung back behind a large family who were squabbling over whose turn it was to use the telescope. Tru lifted up his camera and began taking what he hoped looked like random shots. At least four of them were of Hovy, another four of the people around him exiting the elevator and hanging around it on the observation deck.

"He is not talking to anyone," Sasha said, surreptitiously slipping her hand into her jacket pocket.

Tru caught the gesture and asked nervously, "You didn't pick up a piece back at Fortune's while I was changing?"

"A piece?"

"A gun. A revolver. A pistol."

"You sell weapons in a department store? Only in America."

"Every Fortune's has a fishing-and-hunting department. And you haven't answered me."

"No piece."

"Then what?"

Sasha smiled. "A miniature cassette recorder. Japanese. From your stereo department."

Tru raised his eyes skyward. "Great. Now, even if we manage to convince him you don't have the icon, he can hunt us down for a damning tape."

"He will not know." She gripped Tru's sleeve. "He is coming this way," she warned with nervous anticipation.

Tru scanned the crowd. There was no sign of anyone he recognized from yesterday. Sasha started to step around the still-bickering family, but Tru held her off for another moment.

"Take it nice and slow, Sasha. No accusations. Don't get the guy nervous."

Sasha gave him an impatient look. "Yes, yes."

Even when Bill Hovy stared straight at them, his expression showed no sign of recognition. He was looking for a biker type and a colorless Russian.

He was just about to walk right by them when Sasha murmured, "Mr. Hovy?"

The man literally jumped, blinking several times in a row as he stared at her. "Oh...it is you. You look...different." His eyes then fell on Tru. It was obvious that Tru looked different to him, too.

So did Hovy. He was paler, his features more strained, and Tru guessed he hadn't had much more sleep than he and Sasha last night. Only it didn't look like Hovy had enjoyed himself while he was awake.

The quarters for the telescope ran out and the family walked off. There was no one within earshot.

Sasha leveled her gaze on Hovy. "You remember where we first met?" Sasha asked with deliberate offhandedness.

Hovy nodded.

"Before yesterday at the funeral," Sasha added, ignoring the pressure of Tru's hand on her back.

Hovy shifted nervously. He seemed as concerned about unwanted company as they were. Again he nodded. Sasha was beginning to regret she hadn't opted for a miniature video camera.

"You knew my—" She was going to say "husband," but instead said, "Drew Cheeseman?"

Hovy gave another nod. Sasha grimaced. Tru remained silent, keeping on constant guard for any unsavory-looking characters.

Hovy compressed his lips. A line of sweat beaded his brow even though the enclosed observation deck was airconditioned.

"Spit it out, Hovy." Tru's first words. No one was as surprised as he how effective they were.

"Please," Hovy said with an air of desperation. "I must have it. If it's money you want—"

"I want some answers," Sasha insisted.

Hovy pulled out a linen handkerchief and anxiously began dabbing his forehead. "I know very little. I only know . . . if I don't hand the item over to Martin's associate, I'm . . . dead."

"Dead?" Sasha echoed.

Tru cut in. "How do we know you're not Martin Baker, alias Drew Cheeseman's associate? How do we know—"

"Look, I only went along with this business because Martin swore there was no risk to me." He was already whispering, but now he dropped his voice even lower so that Sasha and Tru had to practically stick their ears in his face. "He actually convinced me he'd been recruited by the CIA to go to Moscow undercover as Drew Cheeseman. I thought I was helping a spy. I did it for . . . Deidre."

"She knew about it?" Sasha asked.

"No, no." But then he seemed to shrink a little inside himself. "I don't know."

"So you thought your pal Martin was a spy for the CIA?" Tru cut in.

"At first."

"And when we got married, what did you think then?" Sasha demanded. "Did you not think it odd that a man who was already married—"

"He told me it wasn't a real wedding. That you were . . ."

Sasha almost laughed. "A double agent? Working with him?"

Hovy nodded.

"When did you discover that you'd been duped?" Tru asked.

"Actually . . . not until after his . . . Martin's . . . death. Right after I heard about the . . . mugging, a man telephoned me. He acted as if I knew all about the . . . icon— that I was in on it. I swore I knew nothing. . . ." He sounded desperate. "You've got to give it to me. Or I'll end up like . . . Martin."

Tru felt himself break out in a cold sweat. "So Martin wasn't mugged."

Hovy grabbed onto the telescope for support. "The man on the phone said that Martin had been stupid to think he could get away with a double cross. And he hoped I wasn't as stupid."

Tru took hold of Hovy's sleeve. "Did you ever see this character in person? Did you ever have any face-to-face dealings with him?"

Again Hovy nodded, as all the color drained from his face. "Yesterday. At the funeral. He told me I'd be in the clear if you had the icon. But that if you didn't...we were all dead."

Tru's grip on Hovy's sleeve tightened. "Who is this guy? What does he look like? Why didn't you go to the police?"

Hovy jerked his arm free, then looked around anxiously. "This man isn't alone. There are...others. They're...everywhere. None of us are safe." He backed off as he spoke and before Tru realized what was on Hovy's mind, he bolted into the elevator just as the doors were closing.

Tru and Sasha had to wait for the next elevator, which arrived less than a minute later. When they got down to the street level, they rushed out only to see a crowd gathered around the open elevator next to theirs.

Even before Tru and Sasha managed to squeeze their way through, they knew. With bleak looks, they stared down at Bill Hovy, sprawled out on the floor of the elevator.

A hushed voice just behind them whispered, "Oh, God. The poor man's dead."

7

"COME ON," Tru whispered hoarsely against Sasha's ear.

But Sasha was frozen to the spot. She couldn't take her eyes off the dead man. Curious, frightened, excited tourists wedged her in place. Anxious, querulous voices produced a tense electric charge around her.

Tru gripped her arm. "Let's go, Sasha," he said sharply.

Tru was right. They had to get away. Even now, the murderer might be close by. He might even be posing as one of the crowd of innocent bystanders. What had Hovy said only minutes ago? *There are others. They're everywhere. None of us is safe.*

Tru kept his hand on Sasha's arm as they edged their way out of the crowd. Fortunately, a couple of policemen were running over. Surely, if the murderer was still around, he wouldn't make a move on them now. This was their chance to get away.

Both had the impulse to run, but didn't want to attract undue attention. Instead, they tried to blend in with the other pedestrians, mostly tourists, as they walked through the sprawling Seattle Center complex.

Tru angled Sasha over to the edge of the sidewalk. "Where's a cab when you need one?" he muttered, checking not only the street, but sneaking looks behind him as well, to see if he could spot anyone on their tail. His arm was around Sasha now and he could feel her trembling. He gave her a reassuring smile even though he wasn't exactly brimming with confidence himself.

"We can't leave," Sasha said, with both fear and resignation showing in her face.

"What?" Tru was hardly paying attention, concentrating instead on getting them out of the area. He picked up his pace, dragging her along with him.

Sasha deliberately slowed down. "We're forgetting Deidre. She is coming to the Space Needle...."

Tru had forgotten all about Sasha's meeting with Deidre Baker. He scowled. "What time?"

"One o'clock," Sasha reminded him. "What if—" She paled, pressing against him. She couldn't bring herself to finish the awful thought that Deidre, too, might be murdered.

Tru looked at his watch. It was twelve-twenty. "Maybe she hasn't left yet." He pointed to a building just south of them where many of the tourists on the street were heading. "There'll be a phone inside. We'll try to call her and head her off." Tru hesitated for a moment. "And then I think we'd better call the police, Sasha."

Without a word, she nodded. Yes, this terrible business had gone too far. Sasha agreed that it was truly too dangerous for them to continue on their own. At least she had the Hovy tape to turn over.

Tru kissed her lightly before they started off. "Don't worry, Sasha. It'll all be straightened out. You didn't do anything wrong. We'll make the authorities here and in Moscow, if necessary, see that. I'm sure of it."

Sasha tenderly touched his cheek, her smile wan but resigned. "Never be too sure of yourself, comrade," she murmured.

THE BUILDING SASHA and Tru entered turned out to be the Pacific Science Center, one of those user-friendly museums for kids of all ages filled with dozens of hands-on exhibits like bubble-making machines, rocket ships and dinosaurs. The place was packed with kids screeching with delight and running from exhibit to exhibit while parents frantically chased after them or forgot about them temporarily as they got lost in some of the exhibits themselves. The atmosphere was cheery and festive— one that felt completely alien to Sasha and Tru, who headed straight for an alcove where there was a bank of phones.

Tru found the number in the directory. Sasha dialed. It wasn't easy. Her hands were trembling. After a minute, still clutching the receiver against her ear, she shook her head. "No answer."

"Give it a few more rings," Tru encouraged. "Maybe she's in the shower."

"Perhaps we should go there to her house." A sick feeling hit Sasha. What if they got there only to find they were too late? What if the man who murdered Hovy had gotten to Deidre already?

"By the time we got across town, it would be after one," Tru was saying.

Sasha stared bleakly at him, then hung up. "We must go back."

"To Denver?"

"To the Space Needle."

"Sasha, are you crazy?"

"We cannot simply let this poor woman—"

"Look, Hovy didn't even think Deidre knew anything about this dirty business of her husband's. Why would anyone want to harm her?"

"He was not so convinced. Besides, if she knows nothing, why did she agree to meet me?" Sasha challenged.

Tru had no comeback.

Sasha gripped his arm. "Already, I am responsible for one death, Tru. I cannot—"

Tru took hold of her shoulders and shook her. "Don't talk like that. You're not responsible."

Tears glistened in her eyes. "He was an innocent man. Duped just like me . . ."

"Hovy could have been lying through his teeth. He could have been the one that double-crossed Cheeseman. For all we know he could have been the one that killed Cheeseman. And maybe he'd have killed you, too, once he got what he wanted."

"Then—then who killed Hovy? And why?"

Tru felt drained. "I don't know," he answered slowly. "That's something the pros are going to have to figure out." He went to reach for the receiver, but Sasha's hand lunged out at his wrist.

"No," she said in a sharp whisper.

"Sasha, we agreed—"

"It's him," she whispered. "The Russian."

For a moment, Tru froze.

"Quick. I do not think he has seen us yet." She motioned toward a staircase near the bank of telephones.

They raced up the stairs to the first floor, hurriedly zigzagging around the exhibits and jostling their way through groups of tourists. Tru kept glancing behind to see if they were being followed. So far, so good. Now, if they could just find another way out.

"Oh, no!" Sasha cried, spotting Black Suit.

"Did he see you?"

"No. I don't think so."

"This way."

Tru and Sasha ducked behind a water-wheel exhibit and hurriedly wedged themselves into a large group that was heading en masse through a pair of open double doors. Only after they stepped inside did they realize they were in a planetarium. A voice boomed out from the speakers announcing that the laser show would be going on in ten minutes—at precisely one o'clock.

Sasha knew she had to get back to the Space Needle to warn Deidre Baker she was in danger. She also knew that Tru would never let her go; he'd already told her it was too risky. Tru was hurrying her down the aisle steps, having spotted a pair of exit signs at the bottom of the auditorium.

As they got close to the front row, Sasha deliberately tripped, pretending to sprain her ankle. She let out a sharp cry and gripped the aisle seat.

"What is it?" Tru asked anxiously.

"My ankle. I must sit."

Tru looked over his shoulder. Black Suit wasn't in sight. Maybe they'd been lucky and lost him. "Okay, move in a little," he said, supporting her by the elbow as he guided her into the row of seats.

"Perhaps you should go and phone the police," Sasha told him.

"And leave the Russian to find you? Nothing doing. We stick together, remember?"

Sasha nodded, feeling a flash of guilt. But how much more guilty would she feel if she didn't warn Deidre that her life might be in danger?

At five minutes to one, the doors were shut and the lights went out. After about two minutes of total blackness, a soft blue light suffused the dome.

The instant there was light, Tru looked back to make sure the Russian hadn't managed to sneak in. He breathed a sigh of relief. The relief was short-lived. As he turned to reassure Sasha that they hadn't been followed into the planetarium, he discovered her seat was empty.

As Sasha raced breathlessly down the street toward the Space Needle she blocked everything from her mind but reaching Deidre Baker and getting her out of there *alive*. Getting them *both* out of there alive. She knew Tru would be coming after her, but hopefully, by the time he caught up with her, she'd already be at the Space Needle and have spotted Deidre.

Only when she got close to the elevators that soared up and down the gigantic tower did Sasha panic. Would poor Bill Hovy's body still be there—a ghastly reminder of just how much danger she was putting herself in? There were certainly still swarms of people milling about the area. But when she got nearer, she saw that the body was gone and the elevators were operating as usual.

As she looked around for Deidre Baker, she also searched for any other familiar faces. She saw no one she recognized. It was a few minutes past one. Perhaps Deidre was already up at the observation tower. A cold chill shot through Sasha despite the heat. What if she was too late to save her?

Behind her she heard some people talking.

"Did you hear that a man died in one of the elevators just a short while ago? That's why there's such a crowd now. They closed off the area for about twenty minutes until the ambulance came and took him away. Some people had to give statements."

"How awful. Was he here with his family?"

"I don't think so. I believe he was alone."

"What did he die of?"

"I heard heart attack."

Sasha scowled. She was certain Bill Hovy had not died of natural causes. It would have been too coincidental.

Yet, apparently his death hadn't raised any question of foul play. There must not have been any stab wounds or bullet holes from a silencer. What then?

"No, that wasn't what I heard," another voice broke in. "The police were saying it was drugs. The guy overdosed."

"A drug overdose? That's disgusting. Why would a drug addict even come to a place like the Space Needle?"

"I would think that's obvious. To meet his dealer. To buy more drugs."

"Oh, no. I don't even know if we should...."

Drugs? Certainly, he was not under the influence of drugs when she and Tru talked with him at the observation tower. There was nothing muted or dulled about his manner or speech. How had his murderer managed to dope him in the elevator?

The elevator doors slid open. As a horde of tourists exited and the group around Sasha began making their way into the elevator, Sasha felt a hand grip her arm, holding her back.

She turned, an apology on the tip of her tongue, thinking that Tru had caught up with her.

Only it wasn't Tru.

TRU RUSHED AROUND a family that was strolling down the broad street. He scanned the crowd for Sasha as he ran toward the Space Needle. He must have spotted a half-dozen blondes in white pantsuits. But none of them was Sasha. Sweat was running in rivulets down his face. Besides worrying about her, he also worried about the Russian thug picking up his trail. But then, better his trail than Sasha's.

THE SHORTER, SQUATTER OF the two blue-suited men who'd tried to grab Sasha yesterday, had her arm, and his taller partner was right behind him. Sasha looked around desperately for Tru, regretting having run off on him. If only she'd listened. If only she'd stayed put.

Tru was nowhere in sight, but just as the grip on her arm tightened, she did spot someone she recognized: Deidre Baker. The pretty brunette was over at the ticket counter. Sasha opened her mouth to shout out a warning.

"We don't want any trouble," hissed the shorter Blue Suit, his fetid breath making Sasha feel even queasier than she was already. "And neither do you," he warned ominously.

Sasha tried to break free of him, but now his partner had moved in close, nudging her forward, away from the elevators. She opened her mouth to scream again, but the shorter man jerked her sharply. She tripped just as she felt something jab at her back. A gun? No. It was sharper, more pointed. And then, as a wave of horror rushed through her, she realized what it was—a hypodermic needle. Just like the one that must have been used on Bill Hovy. Just like the one that had *killed* him. In abject terror, she again opened her mouth to scream, but nothing came out. In the next instant, everything got hazy. And then hazier still.

"Excuse me, please. My wife is ill. Claustrophobia. Excuse me...."

TRU WAS GASPING FOR breath as he saw the crowds squeezing into the elevators. He raced from one to the other, trying to spot Sasha. No luck. Maybe she'd caught an earlier elevator and was already up at the observation tower. Finally he managed to wedge himself into the cramped space of one that was just about filled to capacity. But as he faced forward and the doors were about to shut, he caught a glimpse of a blonde in a white jacket and slacks turning into the pedestrian entrance to the parking facility.

SASHA WAS BEING HELD UP by the two Blue Suits who were half lifting, half dragging her in the direction of a dark sedan parked in a deserted corner of the underground parking area. She was vaguely aware she was being abducted, but she felt too weak, dizzy and disoriented to protest in any way. It was all she could do to try not to pass out; she was terrified that if she did, she would never wake up.

The threesome arrived at the car.

"Hold on to her," the short, squat man ordered his taller partner, as he went to unlock and open the rear door.

The taller Blue Suit complained, but grabbed her roughly around the waist, keeping her upright as she swayed precariously.

TRU HEARD MUTTERED curses as he pushed his way through the dense crowds around the elevators and hightailed it to the doorway where he'd spotted Sasha being dragged. He raced down the stairs, saw no one and instinctively headed for the farthest, darkest section of the garage. When he turned the corner he spotted the three of them at the car, their backs to him. Sticking his hand into the pocket of his windbreaker, he did something he'd seen in a hundred movies: He pretended he had a gun. There was a chance in a million that they'd buy it, but it was the only chance he had.

"Okay, pals, hold it right there and nobody'll get hurt." Tru gave it his best Bogie imitation, which wasn't easy, once he saw that Sasha was in some kind of stupor.

The two men turned and glared at him, the shorter one pulling open the car door.

"Just leave the girl, get into your car, and we'll call it even," Tru drawled, hoping the two creeps wouldn't notice that the "gun" poking out of his pocket was shaking a little.

Sasha swayed, nearly folding over. "I think I am going to be sick," she muttered drunkenly.

"That's the oldest trick..." the short, squat one started to say, but his partner seemed anxious, all the same. Tru wasn't sure if he was referring to his phony gun or Sasha's wave of nausea, but all of a sudden, both men were visibly nervous. They stepped closer to the car, the shorter one opening the front door and quickly sliding across to the driver's seat.

The Blue Suit still clutching Sasha appeared shaken. Tru's heart was pounding. "I mean it. Leave the girl or you're—"

Before he could finish the threat, the tall man practically threw Sasha into his arms and ducked into the car beside his partner.

Tru was just giving himself a justly deserved pat on the back, when he heard the strange, sharp pinging of metal against metal echoing off the still-open rear door of the sedan just as it took off, tires squealing.

Tru spun around. It was Black Suit, the Russian. Tru froze as he saw a silencer-fitted gun peeking out of a newspaper draped over his arm. It was over. The jig was up. With Sasha practically unconscious in his arms, they couldn't even try to make a run for it. And here in the deserted corner of the garage, there were no tourists to notice their predicament and call for help.

The Russian was less than ten feet from them. Tru gathered Sasha in his arms and backed away from him. "Listen, I don't know who you are or what you want from us, but you're wasting your time."

The Russian didn't seem to think so. "Please do not be alarmed," he said in a conversational voice, which, under the circumstances, gave the remark a particularly ominous tone.

Well, now they were as good as dead, Tru thought. But to his amazement he saw Deidre Baker, gun in hand, sneaking up behind the Russian. Stunned, Tru watched her clobber the Russian on the back of his head with the butt of her pistol.

The Russian gasped and then collapsed in slow motion to the ground. Deidre stood still, stunned by what she had done. But when the man began moaning, she regained her nerve.

"Hurry. He'll come to in a minute," she ordered. "I've got my car close by."

Tru hesitated, staring down at Black Suit.

"Hurry," Deidre pleaded.

Tru did, but first, shifting the near-comatose Sasha in his arms, he bent down and swiped the gun out of the Russian's limp hand.

SASHA HEARD HERSELF breathing—in raspy, shallow gasps. Slowly, other sounds began to penetrate. First, just a hum, then after some uncalculated time, voices.

"I think she's coming around." The voice was masculine, tender, familiar.

"Try giving her another sip of water."

Sasha didn't recognize the woman's voice. She blinked several times, but everything was still blurry. She felt a strong arm slip beneath her. Her head lolled against a broad shoulder. A moment later, the cold rim of a glass pressed against her lips but she waved it woozily away. It was almost as if she were underwater and if she swallowed, her lungs would fill with the water and she wouldn't be able to breathe.

"Please, baby. Just take a sip. You're okay now."

"Tru?" She knew it was him, but she wanted more reassurance.

"Yes, baby. I'm here," he crooned, as his arms enfolded her, cradling her, rocking her.

Tears pricked at her eyes as she pressed her face into his chest. "Those...men... A needle... Drugged... Just like..." She clutched at Tru, trembling.

"No, Sasha. Not like...Hovy."

Sasha's head was beginning to clear a little. It was a miracle—a miracle that she was still breathing.

Tru continued to hold her close. "They shot you up with a sedative. A doctor examined you. He said you'd be groggy for a few hours and probably have a wicked hangover."

"I cannot feel my head as yet," she said dryly. "I was afraid I never would again."

He smiled. She was coming around.

"They just drugged you so you wouldn't put up a fight. I'm sure they had every intention of keeping you alive. Until—" He stopped, again shifting his gaze to Deidre, who was standing at the foot of the bed, dabbing at her eyes.

Sasha drew back from Tru, the movement making her head spin—and then throb. He laid her gently down on the pillows as she surveyed the bedroom. "Where are we?"

Deidre Baker came closer. "You're at my apartment," she told Sasha gently.

Tru stroked Sasha's cheek. "We're safe and sound, thanks to Mrs. Baker."

"Deidre, please," the brunette said with an embarrassed smile. "All I can say is I'm so relieved I brought Martin's pistol along. Not that I could ever have . . . shot anyone with it. I have no idea how to use the gun. I've never so much as shot a tin can."

"What made you decide to bring it along?" Tru asked.

Deidre didn't respond right away. "It was because of Bill, really," she replied in a low, sad voice. "Bill Hovy."

Struggling against the grogginess and the pounding in her head, Sasha attempted to follow the conversation. She squinted at Deidre. "He told you that you were in danger?"

Deidre flushed. "Not exactly. I told him I was going to meet you at the Space Needle and he . . . acted very strangely. He said I wouldn't want to talk with you, that it would only upset me. He—he said he thought you were-" she gnawed at her lower lip "—suffering from delusions and paranoia."

Tru turned to Deidre. "Then why did you agree to meet with Sasha?"

Finally, after a lengthy silence, Deidre said hesitantly, "You knew my husband, Martin, didn't you? I mean . . . You knew him . . . intimately?"

"You ask me this question as if already you know the answer," Sasha said quietly.

Deidre clasped her hands tightly together. "He spoke the name—your name . . . Sasha—in his sleep." She began to wring her hands. "When a man sleeps beside his wife and whispers the name of another woman . . ." Her voice trailed off.

"I did not know he was married," Sasha stated honestly.

Deidre nodded slowly, but Sasha wasn't sure she believed her.

"Did your husband know he talked in his sleep?" Tru asked, wondering what else he might have said.

"He didn't do it very often. And he hadn't done it for . . . a long time." They shared a knowing look, and Tru flashed a sympathetic smile, even though he guessed that if Deidre Baker spoke in her sleep, her husband might have heard her murmuring the name, Bill Hovy. Well, what was good for the goose, he supposed. And in this instance another adage came to mind: *Which came first? The chicken or the egg?* Had Deidre already begun her fling with Hovy before Martin Baker began whispering Sasha's name in his sleep? Had he found out? Did Deidre think she'd driven her husband into the arms of another woman? Was she now filled with remorse and guilt?

Sasha, too, had many questions she wanted to ask Deidre Baker, but her headache had taken a definite turn for the worse. She felt as if someone had funnelled a bottle of Russian vodka down her throat. She turned her head and moaned loudly.

"What is it?" Tru said anxiously.

She tried to smile, but it came out more like a grimace. "My head . . ."

"You must rest," Deidre broke in. "The doctor said sleep was the best antidote."

Tru agreed in principle, but he wasn't sure sleeping here in Deidre Baker's apartment was such a smart move—for any of them. Which was what he said.

Deidre nodded slowly. "Can you tell me what this is all about? First, Bill—"

"No," Tru corrected. "First, your husband."

Deidre blanched. "Martin? But he was . . . mugged."

Tru regarded Sasha, who mercifully had once again slipped into a drugged sleep. "Listen, Mrs. Baker . . . Deidre. It's all pretty complicated and I don't know most of the answers myself. And maybe, for your own protection, you shouldn't either. I don't honestly know if you're in any danger, but there's no question about Sasha. I'd better get her out of here before you're linked with us."

Tru hesitated. "You don't know what any of this is about, do you, Deidre?"

"No," Deidre answered in a low voice. "And maybe you're right. Maybe I don't want to know."

"The Russian has no idea it was you who clobbered him so he won't know who to blame. Still, if I were you, I'd be . . . careful. Maybe even go away for a while."

"It's funny you mention that. After the funeral I made plans to go see an old sorority sister in Portland and have a good cry."

"That's fine." He bent down and lifted Sasha into his arms. She fell limply against him, one arm pressed into his chest, the other dangling from her side.

"Wait," Deidre said. "Where will you go?"

Tru hesitated.

"What if something else happens? What if I need . . . your help?" Deidre asked beseechingly.

Tru felt like a heel. Here, this perfect stranger had saved their lives, even though she thought that Sasha had been her husband's lover, and he was still worried about whether he should trust her.

"We're at the Danford Hotel, downtown. We're registered under the name Parks. Mr. and Mrs. Parks."

Deidre smiled gratefully. "Thank you, Mr. *Parks*." She glanced at Sasha, who was still in a deep sleep. "And Mrs. *Parks*. You make a very nice-looking couple."

Tru smiled awkwardly, more acutely aware of Sasha's dead weight as he crossed the room. He was almost at the door when Deidre's anxious voice brought him to a halt. She was at the window, looking down on the street from her twelfth-floor apartment. "Wait. Maybe someone is watching my building."

Tru shifted Sasha in his arms. She was coming around again. "What is . . . happening?" she asked groggily.

Tru wished he had an answer for her.

Sasha's arms went around his neck and she pressed her lips against his cheek. "Mmm, this is nice," she murmured tipsily. "Tell me another joke, Tru."

Tru smiled crookedly at Deidre. "She's delirious."

Deidre smiled back—but only for a moment. "Listen, maybe it's too dangerous for you to stay in Seattle. This Russian may have friends who'll be looking for you at the hotels in town. I have an idea. A friend of mine has a cottage on the islands. She's away on business for the month and she left me the key." Deidre looked down. "Martin and I had planned to spend some time there. It's very private."

"The islands?" Tru asked.

"Yes. San Juan Island. It's just about fifty miles from Seattle. You can get there by ferry." She rushed over to a small desk in the corner of the room, quickly scribbling directions on a piece of paper. Then she grabbed her purse, extracting a key ring. Plucking two keys off the ring, she brought them and the paper over to Tru.

"Here. This one's the key to the cottage and this is the key to Martin's Porsche coupe. It's in the garage under the building, the first stall to the right of the elevator." She stuffed them into Tru's jacket pocket.

"Why are you doing all this for us?" Tru asked suspiciously.

Deidre's eyes rested on Sasha, who had drifted off again. "I believe," she said gently, "it is what Martin would have wanted me to do. You probably guessed that Bill Hovy and I were lovers." Tears ran down her face. "Poor Bill. I was very fond of him, but . . . it was Martin that I loved." She smiled wistfully at Tru. "Love makes us all do incomprehensible things at times."

Tru nodded slowly. How true that was.

8

ALTHOUGH THERE WAS AN interstate to Anacortes, twenty miles north of Seattle, where the ferries docked for San Juan Island, Deidre had named a slower, but much less traveled route up Highway 20. Tru thought it a wise choice, figuring that if they were followed, it would make it easier to spot whoever was tailing them.

Sasha stirred as the Porsche was hugging the narrow road that cut across picturesque Whidbey Island, a short distance south of Anacortes. It had begun raining just as they'd left Seattle. Now the windshield wipers were working overtime, the rain having turned into a full-fledged storm. They were crossing a bridge at the north end of the island when Tru's attention was drawn to a sign that read, Deception Pass State Park. He gave a dry laugh.

Sasha opened her eyes, but closed them almost immediately because of the pain shooting across her forehead. She tried again, this time more slowly. "Where are we?"

"At Deception Pass," Tru said sardonically.

Sasha squinted. "Deception . . . ?"

He reached across and stroked her cheek. "How are you feeling?"

"If I have two heads, I am feeling fine. If not—awful." She looked around at the cream-and-white interior of the lush sports car, then out the rain-spotted window at the turbulent ocean and island-dotted scene, and again at

Tru. "Where are we going? What happened to Deidre Baker? How did you manage to get me away from those two awful men? Whose car is this? Oh Tru, you did not steal it, I hope."

He grinned at her. "Is this the face of a crook?"

Her "two heads" were starting to merge and she actually did feel, if not quite human, almost. "No. It is a most lovable face, comrade."

Tru's grin turned into a nervous smile. Everything had been happening so fast—too fast to think; way too fast to pull out. And now, what was making it really perplexing, he wasn't sure he'd pull out if he could. Maybe he didn't know what the hell he was doing here in a murdered man's Porsche with a drugged Russian beauty that smugglers in Seattle were desperate to get their hands on, but the truth was there was nowhere else he'd rather be right now. He felt a sharp twinge of arousal, but he cautioned himself it was just his adrenaline working overtime; that once this crazy, exciting business got resolved and he had a chance to calm down, he'd be able to put everything—including his intoxicating comrade—into proper perspective. Not that it was the least bit clear how and when that was going to happen.

Sasha's voice jolted him from his disturbing thoughts. "Tru, you were telling me about Mrs. Baker, and how in the world we ended up in this car, in this place."

"Deidre Baker's fine. She'd lending us a friend's cottage on San Juan Island. As well as the car. We both thought it would be a good idea to get you out of Seattle. Once we're settled, we'll call the Seattle police, maybe the FBI and the CIA, as well. I figure one or more of them will know what to do." He hesitated. "I sure as hell don't."

Sasha's hand moved to his thigh and she rested her head on his shoulder. "Poor Tru. You should never have boarded the plane with me in Denver. I have caused you much trouble, yes?"

Tru couldn't argue that, but he rested his hand over hers. "Yeah, you're trouble, all right. With a capital *T*. But, trouble's my middle name, sweetheart," he drawled, Bogie-style.

She lifted her head, his tone jarring a bit of her memory. "You . . . saved me from those two awful men. I remember now. They dragged me to their car in the garage. After they . . . drugged me. But then you appeared and demanded they let me go. You had a . . . gun."

Tru smiled crookedly, a Bogie smile. "Naw, sweetheart, that was no gun. I was just glad to see ya."

It took a few moments for Sasha to get the joke, but then a ripple of laughter burst from her lips. Tru grinned. "You're catching on, sweetheart. One of these days you'll have to tell me some Russian jokes."

Sasha abruptly donned a grave expression. "Oh, Russian jokes are no laughing matter, comrade."

For a moment, Tru thought she was serious. When he realized she'd just told him her first joke, he broke into surprised laughter, and Sasha laughed with him.

ALL PASSENGERS WERE supposed to leave their cars and spend the trip up in the ship's cabin. The flow of people making their way to the stairs had stopped a while ago. Sasha had dozed off again once they'd boarded the ferry, however, and Tru wasn't about to waken her. Instead, he left her sleeping in the locked Porsche and dashed up to the snack bar to get them coffee and a couple of sandwiches.

Images of the day's events assaulted Sasha's sleep—Bill Hovy warning her that her life was in jeopardy; Hovy splayed out on the elevator floor; the short, squat man in the blue suit hissing in her ear, "We don't want any trouble." She moaned as the memory of the hypodermic pricking her squirmed back into her mind. Never before had she felt so helpless. But then Tru appeared. She smiled in her sleep, feeling a yearning, a stir of desire. In her dream, he was coming toward her, his arms outstretched. As he drew closer, she saw that he was holding something in the palm of his hand. Was it a ring? A wedding ring?

No. No, it was not a ring. The object was much larger. But familiar. Frighteningly familiar. Sasha's heart began to pound against the walls of her chest. It was the icon. The stolen icon. Sasha's eyes shot to Tru's face. She let out a cry of alarm. It was not Tru's face now. It was the face of Drew Cheeseman. He was smiling at her—a sinister, diabolical smile.

She screamed.

TRU WAS JUST A FEW CARS away when he heard the scream. Dropping the cardboard tray of coffee and sandwiches, he went racing for the Porsche, his heart pounding. Sasha flung the passenger door open and leaped out. Fully awake now, but disoriented and frightened, she flew into Tru's arms, sobbing.

He held her fast. "You're fine, baby. Nobody's going to hurt you. I won't let anything happen to you."

Sasha slowly realized it had just been a terrifying nightmare. She drew back. "I am sorry. I do not often cry. Usually I am very strong. It is important that I be strong. It was foolish of me to let those two hooligans grab me. I am most ashamed of myself. I should have been more cautious. It is important that I do not rely on—" Before she could finish the sentence, Tru had taken her into his arms.

"Shut up, comrade," he murmured, and the next moment he was devouring her mouth with a fierce, heated kiss.

The rain was beating a tap dance on the deck as it swept over the ferry. They wrapped their arms around each other in a wordless embrace. Tru protected her from the wind and rain with his body as they stood motionless, locked together as if by magnetic force.

Sasha was shocked by the emotional effect Tru had on her—and intoxicated by the physical response he evoked. A flush spread over her face. She felt safe with Tru. She felt strong with him; confident, tender, happy. She wanted him. Oh, how she wanted him. It didn't matter that they were standing in the hull of a public ferryboat filled with cars, the wind and the rain whipping around them. She hungered for him. She looked about the cavernous hull. Had all the passengers left their cars and gone up to the salon areas of the ferry? She could see no one. The hangarlike area was deserted. Her eyes returned to Tru's face.

The longing Tru saw there was contagious, firing his imagination. His mouth ravaged hers as he pulled her closer.

"Sasha, Sasha," he murmured in a thick voice.

A shuddering thrill went through her as he leaned her up against the fender of the car. She felt her slacks being drawn down her thighs, along with her panties. She let out a little cry as the wet metal of the car touched her bare behind. Oh, this was madness. Insane. Incredible. *I'm losing my mind*, she thought, even as her hand moved wantonly to the zipper of Tru's chinos.

I'm obsessed, Tru thought, but he felt a wild exhilaration as he entered her. He wanted to possess her totally. The feel of her invaded him as he invaded her.

Sasha breathed deeply. She held fast, her knees wobbly. Tru's arms closed tightly around her waist, and their chests heaved in unison. Very quickly, they felt the fierce, powerful, shared explosions of their orgasms and then collapsed against each other.

Neither of them spoke. They just stood there for a long moment, holding each other up, both of them stunned and a little embarrassed by the intensity and impropriety of their lust.

"I think it is wise if we go inside the car," Sasha said stiffly.

"Yes. It's raining out," Tru replied inanely.

They broke apart, both hurrying to put into some kind of order their disheveled clothing.

They glanced at each other once they were properly rearranged and smiled awkwardly.

"I confess there was a time or two back in my youth when I fooled around with a gal in a car," Tru said sheepishly. "But this is my first time *on* a car."

"Never before for me, as well," Sasha said soberly.

Tru nodded, but a faint smile crept onto his face.

Slowly, Sasha's lips, too, curved into a smile. And a moment later, they were falling against each other, laughing.

THERE WERE ACTUALLY OVER one hundred and seventy San Juan Islands in Puget Sound, but only four of them were developed to any extent—San Juan, Orcas, Shaw and Lopez. The islands were named by the early Spanish explorers who claimed the lands for Spain but then never came back. Now, the islands were a popular tour-

ist mecca, especially for boating enthusiasts who spent
their days on the sound sailing through the islands,
docking in sheltered coves and exploring, sunning,
swimming, meditating. Today, though, the islands appeared almost deserted because of the storm. Even San
Juan, the largest and most populated of the four, had a
rainswept barrenness about it.

Tru checked the directions on the scrap of paper Deidre
had given him. "It's just a few miles out to the west."

They drove into Friday Harbor, a beautiful picture-
postcard town. Tru knew it was paranoia, but he kept
checking his rearview mirror to make sure they weren't
being followed. When he saw the one car behind him turn
off, he breathed a little easier.

About a mile from their destination they pulled into a
local convenience store to pick up some food. The clerk,
a tired-looking middle-aged man with ginger-colored
hair, was just about to close for the day on account of the
rain. He didn't seem too thrilled to have customers.

"Don't worry. We won't take long," Tru said, grabbing up a plastic shopping basket and tossing one to
Sasha. "You take the first two aisles, I'll take the last two,"
he told her.

Even though the shop was small, Sasha was quietly
awed by the vast assortment of items filling the shelves.
In Russia, the shelves were always so barren, with the few
canned goods and such, looking a bit lost and lonely.

"How are you doing?" Tru asked a couple of minutes
later as he came up behind her. His basket was filled with
milk, juice, bread, cheese, eggs and a couple of bottles
of wine. Sasha's basket was still empty save for a box of
candles that she thought would be practical, in case there
was an electrical failure due to the storm. Shopping for

food, American-style, had proved more daunting for Sasha than tangling with smugglers.

Tru started grabbing cans of soup, boxes of cereal, tins of tuna fish and such and tossing them into her basket. In less than five minutes they were done.

As the clerk was ringing up and packing their food, Tru put his arm around Sasha. "If it clears up tomorrow, we can rent a boat and go out for a sail around the islands. Have you ever gone sailing?" he asked her.

She shook her head distractedly. "Perhaps tomorrow we must do other, more pressing things."

Her remark jolted him back to reality. Ever since those torrid moments of passion on the ferry, Tru had almost forgotten they were on the lam, hiding out from smugglers from opposite corners of the globe. For a few moments, he'd indulged in the fantasy that he and Sasha were just a pair of hot lovers off on a romantic island tryst. But this was no tryst. And if he didn't start putting the brakes on the romance, he might just find himself hearing a Strauss waltz in his head one of these days!

DEIDRE'S FRIEND HAD GOOD taste in getaway cottages. Her quaint gingerbread Victorian had it all—privacy, a view, space, and classy decor. Tru let out a low whistle as he looked around the grounds. If they'd been having a simple romantic tryst, this would have been the ideal place for it.

Sasha was in the kitchen putting the groceries away in the cherry cupboards when Tru strolled in.

"Need any help?" he asked, plucking the bottle of wine from the marble-topped counter and rummaging in a drawer for a corkscrew.

"Are you hungry?" she asked, concentrating on stacking the soup cans neatly on a shelf.

"Mmm, starved," Tru replied, popping the cork and finding an array of cocktail glassware in one of the cupboards. He poured wine for two and brought one of the goblets over to Sasha.

She eyed it cautiously.

"Oh, you're worried about mixing alcohol with that sedative."

Sasha shook her head. "I believe the sedative has worn off now. I am thinking that perhaps we should not make a toast this time."

He set his glass down on the counter just to the right of her. "Are you having regrets, comrade?" he asked gently.

"To have regrets is a waste of time. To waste time is unproductive. I must not look at the past, but to the future. I will telephone to the authorities in the morning. I tried just now but the telephone is not in service. It must be the storm. So, I will telephone again tomorrow. It is just as well, I think. Tomorrow, I will be able to think more clearly."

She could not quite meet Tru's gaze. "I will tell them about Drew Cheeseman—also known as Martin Baker— Bill Hovy, the Russian provocateur and the two men in blue suits who all desire to obtain the icon. Then I will return to Moscow, turn over the icon and face whatever the consequences might be. So now, Tru, I believe it will be best if we . . ." She was so proud of how well she was doing, but now she faltered. He was standing too close to her. The spacious kitchen seemed to shrink around her, as a pulsating warmth enveloped her.

Tru smiled. In one day she'd seen a dead man, been chased, doped, shot at, nearly kidnapped, made torrid spontaneous love on a ferryboat deck; and later in the same day she was ready to dismiss all that and go marching on to a questionable future.

"Why is it you are smiling? I do not say a joke."

"You're quite a woman, Sasha Malzeva," he whispered, leaning closer like a conspirator. "You don't mind if I leave off the Cheeseman?"

"I do not mind." What she did mind, though, was the way Tru's arms had moved around her, his hands gently kneading the taut muscles of her neck and running down her back. "Please, Tru. We cannot do this again."

"What *are* we doing?" Tru wasn't too sure himself. Ever since he'd set eyes on Sasha, he'd been operating on pure instinct. He kept stroking her.

Sasha could feel her willpower being diminished bit by bit with each caress. It took all of what she had left to push him away. She stood stiffly, arms folded across her chest, the sensual lover transformed once more to the dour proletariat. "I will not allow myself to be corrupted by misguided ardor."

"'Corrupted'? You're saying I'm corrupting—"

Sasha cut him off. "I must not allow this most irresponsible and wholly undisciplined aspect of my nature to continue to take hold of me."

Tru backed off. "So, that's what this has all been about? Irresponsibility, lack of discipline, corruption, misguided ardor?"

She heard the anger in his voice, but that wasn't what disturbed her. It was the hurt. She told herself this was nothing more than his bruised ego. Had he not made it very clear that he didn't want any serious involvement with a woman? Had he not made sure he explained to her this tontine so that she would not indulge in any foolish notions? The trouble was, she *was* indulging in foolish notions. She was practically drowning in them. She loved the way she felt with him. She loved the way he looked at her, touched her. She loved the way he made her laugh. Foolish as it was, she loved the man. But she could not give voice to this emotion. She could not allow such foolishness. She had to learn to conceal it—even from herself.

"There is no future for us, Tru," she said simply. "Whatever it is we . . . feel for each other, it is . . ."

"Pointless? Ill-advised?" he snapped.

Sasha made a move toward him, but he held up his hand to stop her. "No. You're right, comrade. We were both getting way too reckless. Hell, I need a little more discipline in my life, anyway."

"Yes," she agreed solemnly. "This is true."

Tru gave her a sardonic smile, spun around and exited.

SASHA CARRIED THE DINNER tray into the living room where Tru was standing at the large bay window staring out at the rainswept blackness. He was holding a nearly finished glass of wine in his hand. Sasha glanced at the bottle resting on a table nearby. It, too, was nearly empty.

"There is soup, bread and cheese," she said quietly. "You should eat."

He acted as though he hadn't heard her, but a few moments later he turned to her. She was sitting on the couch, napkin laid out neatly on her lap, dipping a piece of bread into her soup. The bread was too soft, and fell into the soup as she lifted it to her mouth. She smiled faintly. "I think this is the terrible bread given to American prisoners, yes?"

Tru didn't respond.

"In Russia, we have the best bread. Thick, dark, hearty bread. My grandmother always joked that for the bread alone she would have chosen the motherland."

Tru finished off the wine in his glass and laughed dryly. "I do believe I am, perhaps, a little drunk, comrade."

"Come and eat something."

He smiled wryly. "Eat, drink, and be merry. That's what we Americans say." Instead of walking in the direction of the dinner tray, he ambled over to the bottle of wine, pouring the rest of it into his glass. He finished it off in one long swallow.

Sasha carried a slice of bread and cheese over to him. He stared at her offering and made a face. "I've tasted Russian black bread. You're right. It's better. I happen to love Russian black bread." He swayed a little and Sasha took hold of his arm.

"Come, sit down," she urged.

He didn't put up any resistance as she guided him over to the couch. He even acquiesced about the bread and cheese. Finishing it, he started on the clam chowder. "You're a fine Russian cook, comrade."

She smiled. "This is not cooking, but I truly am a fine cook. I make the very best blinis in Moscow. And superior *paskha*."

"*Paskha*?"

"It is Russian dessert with cheese and fruits and cream. Very rich. Very sweet."

He gave her a tipsy smile. "I am very rich. You are very sweet."

Sasha raised an eyebrow. "I do believe you are more than a little drunk."

His head sagged against the back of the couch and he closed his eyes. "I do believe you're right. I'm tight, comrade." He waved his arm about. "But I have no re-grets. Why cry over spilt milk?"

"In this instance, spilt wine, yes?"

He squinted and grinned at her. "You're becoming a regular stand-up comic, comrade. Spilt wine. Very funny. Keep it up and we'll have you ready for a gig in the Borscht Belt."

Sasha smiled. "Borscht? I make superior borscht."

"I'm crazy about borscht." He leaned an inch closer to her. "And black bread." Closer still. "And blinis. I'm crazy about blinis." They were nose to nose. "I'm crazy about you, comrade."

Sasha sucked in a breath.

He smiled crookedly. "What do you know, comrade? I seem to be crazy about everything Russian."

Having said all that, he passed out, saving Sasha from having to come up with a response to such a heart-stopping confession.

SOMEONE WAS SHAKING him roughly. Was it the Russian? Had Black Suit tracked them down? Or was it Tweedledum and Tweedledee, the blue-suited would-be abductors?

"Tru. Tru! Wake up!"

He opened his eyes groggily as Sasha's concerned voice broke through his stupor. "What . . . ?"

She pressed her finger to his lips. "I think there is someone in the house," she whispered.

The fear and tension in her voice, not to mention the import of her words, awoke Tru fully. His hand moved to his trousers for the gun he'd swiped earlier from the Russian. No gun. No trousers.

He sat up, finding himself stripped to his boxer shorts in an unfamiliar bed. Last he remembered, he'd been sitting on the couch with Sasha, discussing culinary ecstasies. And maybe some not so culinary. His memory was a little hazy, which he thought was just as well.

"Where are my . . . ?"

Before he finished, Sasha held up the gun. "Is this what you are looking for?"

He extended his hand. She hesitated. "I have had training in weaponry. Perhaps it would be best if I—"

He swiped the gun from her hand. "Karate, shooting. You're a regular one-woman army, comrade," he whispered.

Sasha gave him one of her solemn looks. "I am not saying there are times I do not need assistance."

Tru was about to come back with a snappy retort when they heard the distinct sound of creaking floorboards outside the closed door of the bedroom. He reached for Sasha, motioning her to get into the bed. She didn't understand his plan, but she did what he said.

After flinging the covers over her, Tru moved stealthily across the room, grateful for the rug underfoot to prevent any squeaking sound. He slipped beside the door just as it was inching slowly open. His palms were sweaty and he gripped the gun tightly for fear that it would slide right out of his fingers.

Sasha lay very still, ignoring her pounding pulse and the tight constriction in her chest, forcing slow, even breaths, pretending to be asleep. Now she understood that Tru wanted her to lure the intruder to the bed and then he would spring from behind the door with his gun. . . .

There was a slight squeak of hinges as the door opened a little wider. Tru held his breath, staying as flat to the wall as possible, his index finger coiling around the trigger. If the intruder was smart enough to check behind the door, Tru would be ready for him.

Sasha could hear nothing but the sound of her own amazingly steady breaths, but she could sense a new presence in the room. There was no sound of footsteps, but she could almost feel the air shifting, its texture changing as the intruder slowly approached the bed. Her muscles tightened, not in tension now; in preparation. If Tru wasn't expert with the gun, she would have to spring into action before the intruder made a move. But she had to pick her moment very carefully—or it might be her last.

Tru was thinking about optimum moments, too, also realizing that he wouldn't have many chances. At least the intruder hadn't discovered him behind the door. Now all he had to do was surprise the intruder.

It took all Sasha's self control to pretend sleep as she heard a stranger's breathing mix with hers. Any moment now, the intruder might lunge for her. What was Tru waiting for?

As it turned out, all three sprang into action at the same time. Just as the intruder bent down to grab Sasha, she shot her right foot up and out, catching her would-be assailant in the shin, and Tru flipped on the light switch, leaped out from behind the door, his gun cocked, and said, "Don't move or I'll shut—shoot." He was still a little tipsy—and nervous.

9

THE NOW ALL-TOO-FAMILIAR-looking tall, sinister, would-be abductor in the blue suit let out a muttered curse as he grabbed for his injured leg. He hobbled around slightly as if to confirm the presence of a gun in Tru's hand. Tru gave the gun a little wave while Sasha, fully clothed, sprang out of the bed. Their eyes met for a moment, each giving silent approval of the other's move.

The intruder merely sneered at them. "You two are really beginning to get on my nerves," he said with a Midwestern twang.

"The feeling is mutual, believe me," Tru snickered. He sounded confident, but he was really quite edgy. "Where's your little partner?"

The intruder continued sneering. Sasha moved forward and wrenched his right arm up behind his back in a surprisingly quick and economical motion. A low whine of shock and pain emanated from the man's lips.

"You will call to your partner," Sasha hissed threateningly in his ear, "unless you would like a broken arm, yes?"

"He's not—here. Go see for—yourself," he gasped.

"You two have been like Siamese twins up to now. Where is he?" Tru demanded, positioning himself so that no one could surprise him from the hallway.

"He went after...Bartov."

Tru's eyes shifted from the intruder to Sasha. "Bartov?"

"The Russian?" Sasha asked sharply. "The bulky man in the black suit that has been always one step behind us?"

"He's more than one step behind now," the intruder replied sardonically.

"How did you know we were here?" Tru demanded.

"How do you think I knew? I followed you."

Tru looked dubious. "I saw you and your little pal tear out of that garage when the Russian—Bartov—showed up," he countered. "Somebody must have given you a lead." A cold chill ran down his spine. The only somebody that could be was Deidre Baker. Had those been crocodile tears? Was she her dead husband's partner in crime, after all?

"Yeah, we took off, but we didn't go too far," the intruder was saying.

Tru gave him a close look. "What do you mean?"

"We spotted Mrs. Baker's car out on the street, so we just parked a little ways down and hung around. When you three popped out of the garage and hightailed it in her car, I followed you, and Jerry backtracked for Bartov. And when you left Baker's apartment and headed up Highway 20, I put two and two together and waited for you up in Anacortes at the ferry." He smiled licentiously. "Pretty choppy ride across the sound. But maybe you didn't notice."

Sasha froze, as his words assaulted her like an emotional whiplash. This vile man had been there in the hull of the ferry. He'd been there...watching them when they made love. She felt clammy, nauseated, violated.

Rage and revulsion exploded inside Tru. He'd seen himself in the past as hotheaded, but never violent. Now he was filled with a loathing that made him sorely tempted to use the gun in his hand.

Sasha read Tru's mind. "No, Tru. He is not worth it."

It took Tru a couple of moments to get a grip on himself. Then he moved closer, pointing the barrel of the gun at the intruder's chest. Cautiously, he frisked him, pulling a gleaming blue-black semiautomatic pistol out of a chest holster. "Okay, you slimeball. Who are you? Why are you so eager to get your hands on Sasha?" Both Tru and Sasha knew it had to be about the icon, but the more information they had, the better.

Sasha inched his arm up a little higher to get his cooperation.

"Okay, okay. Quit the strong-arm tactics, huh? My name's Lawrence. Jack Lawrence. And all I want is the little item Baker was originally slated to deliver. He came back from Moscow empty-handed, giving us some story about somebody being on his tail over there. So he told us he got a stooge to follow him out and that she'd be carrying the item on her."

Rage shot through Sasha. *A stooge.* That was all she was to Drew Cheeseman. How could she have been so gullible? So blind to his true nature? How could she ever trust her emotions again? she wondered despairingly.

"Only the 'stooge' didn't show up at O'Hare airport in Chicago like Baker said she would." Lawrence glowered. "We thought for a while Baker had pulled a fast one on us and decided to make a deal with one of our competitors."

"So, you . . . killed him?" Sasha's voice was unnaturally low.

"No. Somebody else got to him first," he quipped callously.

"You mean the Russian? Bartov?" Tru asked.

Lawrence nodded offhandedly. "Anyway, Baker swore his stooge had double-crossed him and kept the icon for herself. We got a positive ID on her and when she—" he glanced over his shoulder "—you—surfaced in Seattle, we figured Baker might have been on the level and that maybe you showed up looking for a buyer. We just wanted to be sure we got first dibs," he finished with a diabolical snigger.

"And Bartov?" Sasha asked, her throat dry and raw so that her voice sounded scratchy. "He, too, wanted 'first dibs'?"

"You got the picture," Lawrence drawled. "So, now what? I promise you, Bartov's out of the running. So, what do you say? Can we make ourselves a sweet little deal and all go home happy?"

"Oh, we'll make a sweet little deal, all right," Tru said tightly. "But I'm afraid one of us here won't be going home happy. One of us here won't be going home at all."

A bead of sweat broke out along Jack Lawrence's brow. "Hey, you don't want to do anything stupid, now. I'm just a small cog in a big wheel. Doing me in won't save your necks. We run a real tight operation and no-body double-crosses us and lives to tell about it. Whereas, if you play it smart—"

Tru cut him off. "We're not going to do you in, Jack, old buddy. We're going to *turn* you in. To the authorities. And then, if you play it smart with them and name names, maybe you'll be able to cut a deal, after all."

Tru motioned Sasha over to him. She was reluctant to let go of Lawrence's arm.

"It's okay, Sasha," Tru soothed. "This bastard's at the end of his rope. All we need now is some rope of our own to truss him up. Then we'll drive him into Friday Harbor, deliver him to the local police and they can hand him over to the feds."

She relinquished her grip on Lawrence's arm, and Tru handed her the gun he'd swiped from him. "Just in case."

She managed a faint smile as she aimed the gun on the intruder, then glanced over at Tru. "You would like first to put on your trousers, yes?"

With all that had happened, Tru had forgotten that he'd been standing there all this time, holding a criminal at bay, in his boxer shorts. He hastily stepped into his trousers, threw on his shirt and stuck his bare feet into his loafers as Sasha held her gun on Lawrence. He was awed that her hand was so steady.

Once he was dressed, he motioned to Sasha that she could go.

She gave him a nervous look. "You will be fine?"

Tru glared at Lawrence, pulling back the safety catch of his gun. "I'll be fine and dandy, comrade." He motioned to the intruder. "Okay, drop to the floor on your stomach, hands behind your back."

When Lawrence hesitated, giving Tru an I-dare-you-to-make-me look, it was Sasha who answered his challenge. Both Tru and Lawrence were left virtually speechless with surprise as her free hand sprang out with pantherlike speed, catching the intruder square in the solar plexus. Tru stood there, awestruck, as Lawrence doubled over, the breath knocked completely out of him. A moment later he dropped first to his knees and then flat out on his belly, hands behind his back, as ordered.

"Nice work, comrade," Tru said with a smile. "Three cheers!" he added, toasting her with an invisible glass.

SASHA FOUND A ROLL of heavy cord in the pantry right off the kitchen. Yes, she thought, this would do nicely. She was just about to take her leave when she heard a faint sound. She quickly turned around, tightening her hold on the gun.

She saw nothing behind her in the small storage room. Standing motionless, she listened. Silence. Was the sound her imagination? Or was someone lurking beyond the door, in the shadows? Had Jack Lawrence lied about coming here alone? Was his partner here with him, after all? Had he taken care of Bartov and then met Lawrence at the ferry? She shivered all over. Had they both been there watching . . . ?

A rustling noise brought her up short. Was it coming from the kitchen? She pulled the safety on the gun and cautiously edged toward the pantry swing-door, inching it open. "Who is there?" she demanded in a low, threatening voice.

There was no reply.

Sasha opened the door a little wider and peered into the kitchen. The room was bathed in predawn murky grayness. The rain was still coming down, drumming a steady beat on the skylight. The rhythmic sound took on an ominous quality as Sasha nervously stole out of the pantry.

As she crossed the kitchen she told herself that what she'd heard had most likely been Tru moving about upstairs. And then a frightening thought assailed her: Had Lawrence somehow managed to overpower Tru? She rushed out to the hallway, calling out even before she reached the staircase.

"Tru? Tru, is everything all right up there?"

"Great" he called out, much to her relief.

But as it turned out, everything was not all right downstairs.

Just as Sasha got to the stairs, an arm lunged out from behind her, coiling around her neck. Taken completely by surprise, Sasha dropped both the gun and the roll of cord, the gun making a clanking sound on the bottom step.

A cry caught like a bone in her throat as she heard Tru call out, "Sasha? What fell? Anything wrong?"

A low, masculine voice hissed in her ear, "Tell him to come down." The voice was heavily accented—a Russian accent.

Sasha's mind fumbled and tripped over itself in a frenzy as she struggled to think of a way to overcome the Russian, or at least to warn Tru.

"Do not even consider doing anything foolish, comrade," Bartov snarled. The arm circling her neck tightened, and for several moments Sasha couldn't breathe at all and she was terrified the Russian would crush her windpipe.

When he loosened his hold, her throat burned and she doubted she could speak even if she'd wanted to. Which she didn't. The longer she could delay, the more suspicious Tru would get—and, hopefully, the more cautious he would be.

Tru did get suspicious. Like Sasha, he immediately thought Lawrence had conned them and that his partner had been here with him, hiding downstairs the whole time. And he thought he was being cautious when he hoisted the smuggler up on his feet, wedged the barrel of the gun into the center of his back, and forced him to the top of the staircase, using him as a shield.

"Sasha." It was all that came out of Tru's mouth as he spied her at the foot of the stairs in Bartov's clutches. A wave of desperation swept over him. So Lawrence's stocky partner, Jerry, hadn't taken care of the Russian, after all. Quite likely, Bartov had taken care of Jerry, instead.

Tru, who was still holding on to Lawrence, could feel the smuggler begin to shake, no doubt realizing he was now sandwiched between a rock and a hard place. But Tru wasn't concerned about Lawrence. At the moment he wasn't even concerned about himself. His only concern was Sasha.

"Let her go, Bartov. She doesn't have it. She doesn't have the icon."

Bartov looked up at Tru. "I find that hard to believe, Mr. Fortune."

Tru had to use every ounce of energy to sound convincing. "It's true. She did have it. She brought it to me. I stuck it away for safekeeping. I wouldn't tell her where for her own protection. So if you want it, I'm the one you're going to have to deal with. And I won't deal unless you let her go."

"So now, the great department-store president is importing rare icons?" Bartov's tone was cynical.

"I also left a note with my lawyer that if anything were to happen to me or Sasha, he was to turn the icon over to the authorities, along with the photos I took of you and your rival gang," Tru warned authoritatively.

Bartov only laughed. "I think you see too many stupid American spy movies," he said laconically, once again tightening his grip around Sasha's neck.

She gasped in pain.

"Don't!" Tru cried out sharply. "Don't hurt her, you bastard."

"You are in no position to give orders," Bartov snapped, but he did loosen his grip a little, much to Sasha's and Tru's relief. "We can make this quite painless if you will cooperate," he said amicably.

For all her fear and discomfort, Sasha gave a dry laugh. Bartov repaid her by grabbing hold of her hair and yanking back hard. Despite the stinging pain, she refused to cry out.

Tru was getting desperate. He had to do something. But what? Even using Lawrence as a cover, he'd never be able to get off a clear shot at Bartov with Sasha in front of him. Or could he?

Bartov second-guessed him. "Throw your gun down over the railing," he demanded. "And, since neither of us have any further use for your hostage, you can toss Mr. Lawrence over, as well."

Tru was stunned by the callous, cold-blooded order. Lawrence, thinking Tru would comply, started to plead with Bartov for mercy. "Listen, she talked. She told me where the icon's stashed. We can make a deal. And I've got some other items you might be interested in. Come on, Bartov . . ."

The Russian snickered. "Your people should not have gotten so greedy, Mr. Lawrence. Russia was off-limits to your group and yet you sent one of your operatives to Moscow. That was very foolish of you. And to have taken that particular icon was most unwise since we had already set our sights on it. And there is nothing we abhor more than being disappointed."

"Look, we can set things right now," Lawrence pleaded, breaking free from Tru's loosened hold and starting down the stairs. "We can square things. . . ."

Sasha felt the hold on her loosen, too, as all of Bartov's attention was drawn to the descending rival smuggler. Her eyes flashed on Tru. She gave a surreptitious nod. If only he would understand . . .

Grass didn't grow under Tru's feet. With a quick nod back, he lurched forward and started down the stairs, shoving into Lawrence's back and sending him careening down toward Sasha and Bartov, who were standing by the bottom step.

Bartov was caught off guard. In his haste not to have the smuggler barrel into him, he moved to jump aside. Sasha used that instant to jam her forearm back into Bartov's rib cage. He let out a loud grunt of pain, clutching at his middle.

Sasha sprang free of Bartov's grasp just as Lawrence smacked into him, and both men fell in a tangled heap to the floor. Tru, who was just behind Lawrence, grabbed hold of Sasha's hand. They literally leaped over the bodies and raced for the front door.

"THE CAR KEYS. DAMN! They're in my jacket," Tru groaned as they got to the Porsche.

Neither Bartov's car or Lawrence's was visible. Both smugglers had been smart enough to park their vehicles out of sight. And chances were, they hadn't left their keys dangling in the ignition anyway.

Dawn was approaching and the rain was still coming down as Tru and Sasha raced for the woods. While it would have been a lot easier to stick with the main road, they knew it would only be a matter of seconds before Bartov and Lawrence untangled themselves and one or both of them came after them by car.

When they were about fifty yards into the woods they saw headlights pop on, and heard a car engine start up.

"Duck," Tru hissed, yanking her down as a beam of light danced over their heads.

A few moments later, the car pulled out.

"Which one of them is it?" Sasha asked in a nervous whisper, still flat on her belly on the ground.

"Does it really matter?" Tru whispered back.

He helped her up, pressing her against a wide tree trunk. They both listened for footsteps among the dried leaves. One of them might have gone searching for them by car, but there was still the possibility the other one had also gotten away and wisely decided to come after them on foot, guessing that without a car, they'd head straight for the cover of the woods.

"Are you okay?" Tru murmured against her ear, brushing back wet strands of her hair.

"I am better now," she said, pressing her cheek against his.

"Listen," Tru said after a couple of moments, his body stiffening.

The crunch of leaves. Sasha heard it, too. He pressed his finger to his lips, then pointed due east.

They moved stealthily, watching for twigs and leaves, trying to proceed as soundlessly as possible. Behind them, they still heard what they felt sure were footsteps. Either Bartov or Lawrence was out there. And the other one could double back in his car any time now, once they weren't spotted anywhere near the roadside.

They hugged the trees as they wove their way east, Sasha clutching Tru's hand. For all her earlier bravery, she now felt drained. She was wet, frightened, disoriented, and profoundly fatigued.

As Tru guided her through the woods, recollections of all she'd been through over the past few days overwhelmed her. She nearly stumbled on a stone, but Tru caught her in time. She gave him a quick, grateful look and he smiled back. It was a small smile, but it buoyed her.

Until they heard a whizzing sound followed by the snap of a branch just a few feet behind them. Tru heard the start of Sasha's scream, clamped his hand over her mouth and pointed to a boulder about fifteen yards to their right. Sasha nodded, swallowing down the scream. Moving as quickly as they dared without their footfalls giving them away, they kept low, darting straight for cover.

They made it to the boulder without incident. Sasha was tense and exhausted, but she forced herself to stay alert. Fortunately, Tru still had his gun. He checked the barrel. Five bullets; five chances. His whole body, already drenched from the rain, broke out in a cold sweat. The muscles around his jaw tightened. He had never shot at a man before in his life—another of many firsts in his life since he'd met up with Sasha Malzeva. But, then, everything about being with Sasha felt like a first.

They could hear the faint rustle of leaves, but when they risked a look, they saw no one. Could they have been lucky enough to run for cover without being spotted? They waited, silent, their muscles taut, their wet bodies flattened against the boulder.

Neither of them had any idea how long they stayed like that. Minutes? Close to an hour? They had lost any sense of time. At some point, though, they stopped hearing the sound of leaves crunching underfoot. Still, neither of them moved, not wanting to take any risks now. The stalker could be out there, as still and silent as they were, waiting for them to make the first move.

Only when his muscles began to cramp, did Tru finally look over at Sasha. "What do you think?" he whispered.

"I do not know. I do not hear anything," she whispered back.

Tru nodded. He raised himself slightly to get a wider view beyond the boulder. He saw no lurking figure. He rubbed his jaw to ease the muscle tension. Then he saw

Sasha bend down and pick up a large stone. He gave her a puzzled look, and she made a throwing motion with her hand. Tru got the idea. Taking the stone from her, he pitched it a good hundred feet into the woods, then ducked back down behind the boulder. A few moments later, he picked up another stone, tossing it a bit farther. If someone was out there and heard the sound of the stones dropping, he might mistake it for footsteps and head in that direction.

Sasha and Tru once again flattened themselves against the boulder and listened intently. After a few breathless moments, they heard footfalls about fifty feet away and as those steps faded into the distance, they realized with considerable elation that their little plan had paid off.

"Come on," Tru whispered, gripping her hand.

The rain was letting up a little as they got to a clearing about twenty minutes later.

"Look," Sasha said, pointing to a small cottage in the distance. "Perhaps they have a telephone and we can call the police."

"If the phones are working yet." But there was one more "if"—if Bartov or Lawrence hadn't got to the cabin first and was lying in wait for them—but Tru left that "if" unspoken. He kept his fear in check, as well.

Sasha squeezed his hand. Their gazes met and held for a long moment. He realized she was thinking the same thing and that she understood his fear—as he understood hers. They didn't need words to communicate with each other.

10

THE SKIES WERE BEGINNING to clear and the rain had reduced to a drizzle, but they were both drenched to the bone, both shivering from the brisk early-morning wind coming off the sound. Later in the day, it would heat up—maybe in more ways than one; and maybe sooner than they expected.

Tru had his hand behind his back, gripping the gun, as he knocked on the door of the cottage. Sasha stood beside him. After what felt like an eternity, the door cracked open and a sliver of a face revealing one brown eye, peered out at them.

"Can't help you till eight," a crabby voice muttered.

Tru tried to place the man. He'd heard the voice before. It was Sasha who remembered. It was the glimmer of ginger hair that did it.

"The man from the grocery store, Tru." She looked past the cottage. About a hundred yards away, right off the road, was the small general store where they'd stopped yesterday to buy their provisions.

"Look, we just need to use your phone," Tru said.

The man didn't close the door in their faces, but he also didn't open it any wider. It was no wonder. They did look a sight—soaked and disheveled; Sasha's white slacks and jacket splattered with dirt and mud, Tru's shirt half-undone, half coming out of chino slacks that had seen better days—only a day ago.

Tru's grip tightened on the gun. There was always the chance that either Bartov or Lawrence was keeping an eye and a gun on the storekeeper from inside the cabin. But somehow Tru didn't think so. There was no sign of fear in what he could see of the man's craggy face—just suspicion and irritation.

Tru knew they couldn't afford to stand out in the open much longer. One or both of their pursuers could show up here any minute.

He glanced over at Sasha and knew she was thinking the same thing. The gun. It was their only option.

He didn't hesitate. If he had, he might not have been able to pull it off. He withdrew the gun. In the same instant, Sasha darted her foot in the opening of the door, one step ahead of the storekeeper's efforts to slam it in their faces.

"Look, don't be alarmed," Tru said quietly. "We're undercover agents. FBI. And we just need to phone into our—"

"Control," Sasha quickly filled in the blank.

The man gave them a guarded look. "Where's your ID?"

Tru could feel the seconds ticking by like a time bomb, but he smiled crookedly. "You don't carry ID when you're undercover," he said reasonably.

When the shopkeeper continued blocking the doorway, Tru waved his gun. "This is my ID," he said a bit ominously.

"Please," Sasha added gently. "We don't want innocent people getting hurt."

He wavered for another moment. "You're Russian, aren't you?"

She nodded, then smiled—a provocative smile.

It did the trick better than the gun.

TRU HAD BEEN ON THE phone for a good five minutes. Sasha, agitated, watched for a sign of Bartov or Lawrence. Fortunately, the cabin wasn't visible from the road, as it sat about fifty feet directly behind the general store, camouflaged by a ring of eucalyptus trees. Even from the woods, the cabin was likely to go unnoticed. Still, it was possible that one of the smugglers might stumble upon it. Time was of the essence, and Sasha listened anxiously to Tru's conversation. He was plainly having problems communicating their perilous situation to an FBI agent back in Seattle.

"I told you, Mr. Milton, I don't have time to go into lengthy explanations," Tru snapped into the receiver, rolling his eyes at the ceiling. "I've already gone over that. Some Russian named Bartov on team A. And two bozos by the names of Jack and Jerry on team B. Jack Lawrence. I don't know Jerry's last name. I don't even know if Jerry's still alive. Bartov might have . . ."

He listened, his expression growing more frustrated. "No, that was the other one. Hovy. Bill Hovy. At the Space Needle. We've got a tape. We're pretty sure that overdose was no accident. I think either Jack or Jerry got him with a hypodermic needle in the elevator. Or maybe it was Bartov. Or . . . Who knows how many others are involved?"

Again, he listened.

"Look, Milton," he said sharply. "We can't stick around here." There was another pause. "Right. If we get out of here alive." Tru slammed the receiver into the cradle, immediately regretting his last comment as he took in Sasha's pale face. The storekeeper's complexion wasn't all that good, either.

Tru crossed over to Sasha, putting his arm around her shoulders. Her clothes were soaked, her hair curling from the wetness. He felt a sharp twist of protectiveness, mixed with desire. "Are you okay?" he asked her softly.

She shook her hair back from her face and managed a smile that looked more winsome than valiant. "I am fine."

He drew her close for just a moment. Her smile took on a new quality, but he wasn't quite sure what it was. Nor did he have time to think about it.

The storekeeper was moving toward a closed door. Tru quickly lifted his hand, pointing the gun at him, giving him a warning look. "Where are you going?"

"To get you a couple of towels so you can dry off a little."

"We don't have time to dry off. We need a lift to Friday Harbor." He wasn't asking, he was demanding.

The man rubbed his jaw, considering Tru's order.

"You have a car, don't you?" Tru said impatiently.

"Got a pickup."

"That'll do," Tru replied, motioning him with the gun toward the front door. "Let's go."

The storekeeper didn't budge. "I don't think so."

Tru felt a rush of rage and exasperation. "Look," he snapped, "I'm not going to stand here arguing with you...."

Sasha gripped Tru's arm, her expression calm and reasonable. "It will be best for you as well as for us to leave here for a while."

To Sasha's and Tru's surprise, the man with the ginger-colored hair nodded in agreement.

Sasha smiled. "Good, then we will all go to Friday Harbor, yes?"

After what felt like an eternity, the man nodded.

"Where's the pickup?" Tru asked quickly. "Out back?"

"In Friday Harbor."

"What's it doing there?"

"Getting an engine overhaul."

Sasha felt an awful desperation set in. "But surely you have some means of transportation, yes?" she asked, feeling tears rush into her eyes.

"Sure. I got a boat. Lot smarter to go by boat to Friday Harbor anyway, I figure. Slim chance those bozos out there got themselves boats. Should be smooth sailing—if you know what I mean."

Sasha laughed. So did Tru.

IT HAD STOPPED RAINING when they reached Friday Harbor. Sasha and Tru thanked the storekeeper profusely as they alighted from the boat. Tru offered him some money but the man refused, giving them an offering instead—a pair of binoculars he had in his boat.

"For whale watching while you cross the sound." He smiled. "Or for bozo watching."

There was a ten-minute wait for the next ferry to Anacortes. While Tru kept guard, Sasha ducked into a gift and souvenir shop, coming back out a few minutes later with gray sweatshirts that read San Juan Island in red across the front, and two long-billed Seattle Mariners baseball caps.

When she had her sweatshirt on and her blond hair tucked up into her cap, Tru grinned. "The all-American gal next door."

She shook her head solemnly as was her wont. "No. Not *all*-American, but one-part American, yes. My grandmother, Leila."

"I think my grandmother was right. You've got a lot more of Leila's genes than you think. And her looks," he said tenderly.

Quite suddenly, she threw her arms around him. "Oh, Tru, you were very brave. I was afraid. I was afraid that...we...would not get away. You were...wonderful."

He held her closer and pressed his lips against her neck. "You weren't half bad yourself, sweetheart." This time the Bogie impression didn't make it. His voice held too much of a quiver, too much of emotion. Sasha didn't have a corner on fear. He'd been plenty frightened himself. Still was.

She drew back. "The ferry is coming." She stared down at the binoculars in Tru's hand. "This time we will only watch for whales and possible bozos, yes?" There was a wistfulness in her smile.

And in Tru's.

LUCK WAS WITH THEM on the ferry ride. Lots of whales frolicking in the sea and not a bozo in sight. Hopefully, Jack Lawrence and Bartov were still combing San Juan Island for them.

As soon as they docked in Anacortes, Tru gestured toward the information booth. "Come on. We'll find out about the closest car-rental place."

Sasha slipped her hand in Tru's, holding him back for a moment. "We will drive back to Seattle and see the authorities, yes?"

He nodded, trying to put as much reassurance into his nod as he could. He added a few words: "It will be okay, Sasha. The guy I spoke to seemed real interested in Bartov and Lawrence. And their cronies. Who knows? Maybe you'll even end up with a reward." He flashed a winning smile—a Fortune smile.

Her eyes seemed to turn a deeper shade of aquamarine as she looked at him. Or maybe it was the reflection of the water. "Promise me one thing, Tru."

He almost said, "Anything," but instead he answered, "Sure."

"You will tell me more American jokes as we drive back to Seattle."

He leaned toward her, touched her chin, kissed her. Then he popped the brim of her baseball cap lower on her forehead and put his arm around her, steering her toward the information booth. "Did you ever hear the one about the farmer's daughter?"

They were almost at the booth when Tru felt a hand come down firmly on his shoulder. An instant later, a hand fell on Sasha's shoulder. They both gasped and whirled around to see two strangers dressed in casual clothes. But there was nothing casual about their manner.

The man who had his hand on Sasha gestured to a gray sedan at the curb. "We've got a car waiting." A powerful scent of floral after-shave emanated from him, making Sasha feel instantly queasy.

Tru's hand made as discreet a move as he could manage for the gun in his pocket, but the man behind him, a couple of inches taller and more than a couple of inches broader, gave his head a little shake. "That would be a real stupid move," he said in a calm but deliberate voice.

Sasha's heart was beating erratically and she could feel the unpleasant heat of the man's hand radiating through her sweatshirt to her damp skin. She chastised herself for having let her guard slip.

Tru was doing some of the same. He told himself he should have been smart enough to realize one or both of the smugglers would have gotten word to their pals on the mainland to keep a lookout for them in Anacortes. And here, only moments ago, he'd been telling Sasha everything would be okay.

There was nothing for it but to let the two bozos lead them to the car where a third bozo wearing a Hawaiian shirt and white Bermuda shorts, was waiting patiently behind the wheel.

After being discreetly relieved of his gun, Tru was hustled into the front seat, and found himself quickly sandwiched between the driver and the burly man who'd tagged him. Sasha was handled with a little more care, and was ushered rather than shoved into the back seat with her "date."

Tru swung around despite being wedged in, and gave the younger, leaner man beside Sasha an icy look of warning. Surprisingly, the man merely smiled pleasantly and moved a few inches farther from Sasha.

"Where are we going?" Tru demanded as the driver pulled out from the curb.

The driver gave the man on the other side of Tru a quick look first to get his okay. "Seattle."

"And what happens when we get there?" Tru asked, keeping his head angled so that he could keep one eye on the guy in the back seat and make sure he kept his distance from Sasha. Tru didn't know exactly what he would do if the guy didn't, but he knew he would do something. Sasha smiled at him, as if to reassure him that she would be okay. It took a conscious effort.

The burly man beside Tru was looking at him closely. "You said you wanted to talk, Mr. Fortune. I assume you—" he included Sasha in his gaze "—haven't changed your minds."

"You assume? Who the hell are you?"

The burly man smiled enigmatically. "We just talked on the phone a few hours ago, Mr. Fortune."

Tru's eyes narrowed. "You mean you're the guy I spoke to at the FBI office? Milton?"

"Special Agent Frank Milton, Seattle Division." He motioned toward the driver. "Special Agent Lou Bonfiglio. And that's Special Agent Barry Fleming, seated beside Mrs. Cheeseman—"

"She isn't Mrs. Cheeseman," Tru retorted, cutting him off.

Special Agent Milton gave Tru a wry smile. "Right. She's just some cute little number you picked up on the ferry."

"She was never married to Cheeseman," Tru said wearily. "It was a con. There never was a Cheeseman. His name was really—"

"Baker?" Milton offered. "Martin Baker?"

"Right," Tru muttered, then gave him a desultory look. "You might have identified yourselves back at the dock. We thought you were with them."

"With whom?" Milton asked.

Tru shrugged. "Good question. I don't know. There are at least two different groups after the icon. For all I know, there could be others."

Milton gave Sasha a questioning look. Sasha stiffened, but said nothing. A cold chill went through her and it had nothing to do with the air-conditioning in the car and still being damp. This was the beginning of the interrogation. She must steel herself for it. Despite Tru's reassurances, Sasha was terrified. Would she be accused of wrongdoing?

She was grateful when Milton turned around without pressing her for answers. He flicked on the radio. She was surprised at first that he asked no more questions, either of her or Tru. But then she surmised that these agents were not the official interrogators. They were merely delivery boys. Back in Seattle, others waited for them. Agents, no doubt, who were higher ranked. Then the true "grilling" would begin.

Tru, too, surmised that the three men had merely come to pick them up and take them safely back to Seattle. He wasn't thrilled with the way they'd introduced themselves, but he felt none of Sasha's terrors. He was confident that she wouldn't be implicated and was greatly relieved to finally be able to set things straight, get her safely away, and let the pros finish the job.

THEY ARRIVED IN SEATTLE in the early afternoon. There was a misty drizzle, but after all the drenching rain they'd experienced, this sprinkle went unnoticed and Tru and Sasha were a bit amused when the agents popped open umbrellas to shield them as they were escorted into an office tower downtown.

"I'm sure you'd both like to shower and change your clothes," Milton said as they stepped inside the lobby. "We stopped at your hotel earlier to pick some stuff up for you, but there wasn't much there in the way of apparel."

Or anything else, Tru knew the agent was thinking. Like an icon or two. And then he thought of something. "How did you know where we were staying? I didn't mention it on the phone."

Sasha felt her muscles constrict. "You have been following us?"

"Indirectly," Milton replied. "We'd been keeping an eye on Martin Baker—"

"You must have blinked a lot," Tru said sardonically.

Milton motioned them into the empty elevator, then stepped in after them, along with his partner, Fleming. The agent in the Hawaiian shirt had remained in the car.

"Like I said," Milton continued after pressing number fourteen, "we'd been watching Baker, but he had a way of giving us the slip. If he hadn't been so good at it, he'd probably still be alive."

"And behind bars," his mostly silent partner muttered.

Milton gave Fleming a sharp look. "Anyway, after he got taken out, we kept an eye on his close acquaintances and his wife." He smiled awkwardly at Sasha. "His real wife. Deidre Baker."

"And Deidre told you what hotel we were staying at here in Seattle?" Tru queried.

Milton stared up at the blinking numbers over the elevator doors. They were getting close to fourteen. "No, not exactly. She dropped by your hotel room last night. Of course, we didn't know it was your hotel room right away. But when we showed a photo of you, Mr. Fortune, to the desk clerk, he recognized you immediately."

Tru and Sasha shared puzzled looks. Why had Deidre Baker gone to their hotel? Obviously not to see them, since she'd sent them off to San Juan Island. There was only one conclusion they could draw: She must have gone looking for the icon, hoping they'd stashed it in their hotel room and couldn't risk retrieving it before escaping to that nice, supposedly safe little oasis across the sound. The next question popped into their heads at the same time. Was Deidre acting independently or was she a member of a ring? And which one? Most likely not Bartov's group, since she'd kept him from nabbing them in that parking garage. But it made sense that she was working with Jack Lawrence....

"I'LL BET ALMOST ANYTHING she's in cahoots with Lawrence," Tru was saying to Special Agent Ron Waterman, a tough haggard-looking middle-aged man who actually bore a faint resemblance to Bogie.

"You could be right," Waterman remarked without much animation.

"It fits," Tru went on. "Lawrence didn't just put two and two together when we took off for Anacortes. The goon probably doesn't even know how to add. No. He knew exactly where we were heading because Deidre Baker told him." He rubbed his jaw thoughtfully. "And that's probably how Bartov knew where to find us, too."

Waterman scratched at his five o'clock shadow, which was already visible even though it was only a few minutes after two. "I don't get it. Why would she tell Bartov if he's not on her team?"

"She did not tell him. It was most likely Jerry, Lawrence's partner, who told Bartov, in hopes of saving his life," Sasha said, a brittle edge in her voice.

Tru reached across to Sasha and took hold of her hand. It was as cold as ice. "Look," he said, turning to Waterman, "why don't you bring Deidre in for questioning? Wheedle the truth out of her. She's the key—"

"She's missing."

"Missing?" Tru and Sasha exclaimed in unison, exchanging nervous looks.

Waterman cast a narrow glance over at Milton and Fleming, who were hanging out near the office door. "She gave my boys the slip after she left your hotel."

Tru threw up his hands. "So, now what? We've got Deidre, Lawrence, Bartov and who knows how many others on the loose, all looking to get their hands on Sasha."

Sasha squeezed his hand. "You are no more safe than I am," she said softly.

Tru gripped Sasha's hand tightly. "Look, we told you all we know. And Sasha's only too happy to tell the Russian authorities where she's been stowing that damn icon for safekeeping. So, why don't you boys all get together and round up the smugglers while I take Sasha away from this craziness and off to someplace really safe?"

Before Waterman could answer, Sasha interrupted. "I cannot do that, Tru. It is my responsibility to help in any way I can to bring these criminals to justice. I cannot turn my back—"

"This isn't your problem," Tru argued. "And it isn't your profession."

Sasha looked at Waterman. "If you do not arrest me or return me to my homeland to face charges," she said resolutely, "I will offer you whatever assistance I can."

Waterman smiled at her. "I appreciate your offer, Miss Malzeva. Now, back to business. You've given us a fairly detailed rundown," Waterman said laconically, glancing over at the tape recorder on his desk.

"Well, maybe you ought to play it back, because it obviously didn't penetrate," Tru snapped.

"Please," she said to the chief interrogator. "May I have a few minutes alone with my... friend?"

Waterman rubbed his palms together. Finally, he gave Sasha a nod, then nodded to his two underlings.

A minute later, Tru and Sasha were alone in the office. Tru got up from his chair and pulled Sasha up from hers, grasping her shoulders firmly. "You've got to look out for yourself here."

"You are saying this because you are frightened for me, Tru."

He started to argue, but then his whole demeanor changed. He felt a constriction in his chest and pulled her roughly to him, burrowing his face in her hair. "You're damn right, I'm frightened. I don't know what I'd do if anything happened to you, Sasha." He shut his eyes tightly. How had all this happened to him? How had he arrived at this juncture? How had he come in so short a time to feel so much, to care so much? To love this utterly impossible, irrepressible woman so much?

She drew back, and looked up into his eyes, as tears slid down her cheeks. "We will never waltz together, Tru, but I will never forget. When I am back in Moscow and you are once again the important business tycoon back in Denver, I will think of our time together and sometimes I will...laugh. And it will feel so good, Tru. But right now, I cannot laugh. Not now, when we must say...goodbye."

A cry of anguish escaped his lips as his mouth sought hers. He pulled her close, pinning her arms to her sides, and kissed her hard and fast, feeling her whole body quake as she gave herself up to the kiss. But then he abruptly drew her back from him, shaking her a little. "Hell, you think you're the only one with a political and social conscience? Well, you're wrong. I've got as much conscience as the next guy, and I'm not leaving until those bastards are all put behind bars. So there." A slow smile curved his lips. "Besides, I've still got a few more good jokes to tell you." He touched her cheek and plucked the baseball cap off her head, so that her hair cascaded down around her shoulders. Then he slipped his hand around the back of her neck. "And something tells me we're going to need a few more laughs before this is over."

"Yes," she murmured. "I would very much like a few more laughs before this is . . . over."

11

"SO THIS IS A SAFE house?" Tru mused, an ironic smile on his face as he surveyed the tiny studio apartment in one of Seattle's less illustrious neighborhoods—an old section of town that was obviously still in the planning stages of redevelopment.

"Not exactly the Ritz, I grant you," Agent Milton said defensively. He knew Truman Fortune was used to better—a lot better.

Sasha was too distracted to care. Her surroundings were of no interest to her at the moment; her mind was on more serious matters.

"At least," Milton quipped, "you won't be bothered here."

Tru gave him a narrow look. "You haven't said how we're going to be of assistance yet in tracking down these assorted smugglers."

Milton rubbed his scratchy face, his five o'clock shadow now a thick, dark stubble. "That's for the big brass to decide. Don't worry, we'll be in touch."

"Right. Why worry?" Tru replied dryly.

Milton nodded. "In the meantime, like I said, you won't be disturbed. Of course, if you want . . . more privacy—I mean, for each of you—there's another studio apartment with a connecting door through the kitchen." He shuffled his feet. "Just let me and Fleming know. We'll be upstairs."

"Just the two of you are on guard?" Tru asked, sounding dubious.

"Oh, no. There's two more boys downstairs. And a new crew will come in for the night shift. We've got the place secured. Besides, no one but our people could know you're here."

"That hasn't stopped those bozos before," Tru retorted.

"Believe me, you'll be as safe as babes," Milton concluded.

"Look, in the distance," Sasha exclaimed, moving to the window. Tru and the agent followed her there. "You can see the Fortune's sign on the rooftop. That is the store we shopped in, yes?"

"Oh, right. Clothes," Milton said. He signalled to his partner, Fleming, who was standing by the door. "They'll need some stuff."

"Waterman said he'd have someone in the office pick them up a few things and deliver them before our shift was over."

"How come Waterman never tells me anything?" Milton muttered irritably.

Fleming crossed the room to a louvred-door closet. "There's some stuff in here." He pulled out a print sundress and a frilly blue-and-white-striped blouse hanging over a white pleated skirt.

Tru gave the clothes the once-over, then looked derisively over at Fleming. "What happened to the gal who used to own those things?"

Fleming shrugged. "Wasn't our assignment."

Tru smiled thinly. "Probably just as well." He had little faith in a pair whose assignments had been Martin Baker and his wife, Deidre, both of whom had managed to give the boys the slip. Not that getting away had done

Martin Baker any good. And for all Tru knew, maybe not Deidre, either.

"NEED A HAND?"

Sasha smiled provocatively as she stood under the spray of the shower. "I need more than a hand," she murmured, pushing the plastic curtain aside so that Tru could step into the tub.

He stood facing her under the spray, a smile dancing on his lips. "I wanted to do this that first night in Denver. In that cabin. A popular saying we have whenever there's a drought kept playing over in my mind: Save Water And Shower With A Friend."

"I like this saying very much," she said huskily.

He sighed, transfixed by the sight of her lush body. "You're so beautiful, Sasha. Everything about you . . ."

"I like also the saying, Never Judge A Book By Its Cover," she murmured. Warm water was streaming down his face. Her hand grazed his wet cheek.

He grinned. "We both did that, didn't we?"

She laughed. "I thought you were a . . . Hell's Angel, and you thought I was . . ."

His mouth covered her open lips.

"What we thought doesn't matter," he said when they broke apart. "It's what we think now. What we feel. I'm never going to forget one moment of this adventure, Sasha." He pulled her glistening-wet body to him, flattening her high, firm breasts against his chest. He wanted to say that he would never let her go, but that would have been a lie. As soon as this adventure was over, Sasha would return to Moscow and he to Denver. For each of them, the risks of any other plan were too great. Sasha had been badly burned once and she needed time to heal. And her heart belonged to her homeland. As for Tru, his heart belonged to Fortune's—and to everything that went with it: the wealth, the power, the obligations, the responsibilities, the plans for the future.

Still, he couldn't let her go just yet. "I don't know, Sasha. Maybe if things had been different... Maybe..." Silently, he cursed the tontine. *For the first time.*

Her lips were at his ear. "It is best this way, Tru. For us, there is only now, my darling, my true love," she whispered as the steamy water inundated them. Her hands slithered provocatively down his wet, muscled body. He was already hard as her fingers encircled him. The wondrous feel of him enthralled her.

Tru was mesmerized by the erotic movements of her hand, and then when she knelt down in the tub, her mouth continuing the sensual ministrations, a breath whooshed out of him with an audible rush. His thighs began to tremble as all thought was blotted out by an inundation of vibrating pleasure.

He drew her up, kissing her hard and deeply. Then he picked up the soap and began lathering her body with slow, sensual and deliberate movements. She tilted her head so that her wet hair cascaded down her back as he soaped first her long slender neck, then her firm breasts, their nipples already hard. He bent down as he moved to her narrow waist, then her gently flaring hips. She let out a sharp gasp of pleasure as his soapy hands trailed between her legs, up and down, up and down.

She felt a kind of ecstasy in the way he touched her body. His caresses were so tender, erotic and knowing. Her breathing grew shallow as he gently, deftly probed between her thighs, the soap and water running down her body now as he guided her under the spray.

"Turn around," he murmured softly.

And as she did, he began his wondrous, sensual assault on her back, her spine, her buttocks, the backs of her legs. She felt so weak, she had to press her palms against the tile wall to support herself.

Then his hands gently turned her around to face him again and she fell helplessly against him. She was on fire, burning, burning. . . .

"Yes, now. Now, now, now." She wasn't sure if she'd said the words out loud as his hands slipped under her arms and he hoisted her up, pressing her against the wet tiles. They kissed for a timeless moment and then he entered her. Their eyes were open, each delighting in watching the play of passion and pleasure on the other's face. But finally their eyes fluttered closed as they gave themselves up to pure, sublime sensation.

In the end they collapsed to the bottom of the tub, enveloped in the warm water and rising steam.

SHE STOOD AT THE WINDOW dressed in the print sundress left in the closet by an anonymous woman, her golden hair shimmering as the setting sun bathed her in a soft glow. She contemplated the Fortune's sign in the distance, while an idea that had begun to blossom earlier in her mind took hold.

With sudden resolution she spun around. Tru had opened up the convertible sofa and was stretched out on what was now a queen-size bed. His eyes were on her and she sensed he'd been watching her the whole time.

She wanted to blurt out what was on her mind, but something held her back. Instead, she found herself asking, "What are you thinking?"

"Do you know how much I want to touch you at this moment?"

She smiled. "You are . . . insatiable, yes?"

"Yes." He patted the bed beside him.

She did not move.

"I never did finish telling you the joke about the farmer's daughter," he whispered seductively. "Come lie beside me, Sasha. Let me make you laugh. I love to see you laugh."

"Tru." She needed to discuss other matters, but she knew that to do so would shatter the magical mood. And there would be so few magical moments for them. And yet . . .

He sat up, observing her closely. "Okay, comrade. No jokes." Now the word *comrade* was spoken as an endearment, the sound shaded in tenderness and warm affection.

"I do not think it would be wise to wait for this Waterman and his colleagues to devise a plan. They do not know the players as we do. We must have a plan of our own, Tru. We must draw all of the players out. Trap them."

He scowled. "And I suppose you have a plan." It wasn't a question.

She smiled. "Fortunately, yes."

Tru sighed. "I don't suppose it would do any good to tell you that the feds have done this sort of thing before and have probably got a plan of their own up their sleeves by now?"

She didn't respond, but then he didn't really expect her to.

Tru sighed. "I guess you'd better spit it out, because whatever it is, we're in it together."

"Do you remember, yesterday, the display in the men's clothing department on the main floor at Fortune's?"

Tru rubbed his jaw. "The display? In the men's department?" He tried to picture what it was, but he drew a blank. He'd only seen it in passing, his concentration having been focused on ushering Sasha as quickly as possible across the main floor of the store to the elevator. He was amazed that she had noticed it.

"Gangsters. The mannequins were all dressed as gangsters. And there were signs marked Prohibition, Speakeasies...."

Now Tru remembered. "Right. It's a 1920s theme. The clothing's a takeoff on the kinds of fashions worn then by mobsters like Al Capone and Bugsy Siegel. We've actually got a similar display in several of our stores. It's the hot new fashion." He gave her a puzzled look. "What about it?"

Sasha slowly crossed to the bed, a conspiratorial smile playing on her face. It was a smile that made Tru very nervous.

WATERMAN'S FACE CRINKLED thoughtfully. "It's a pretty crazy idea."

Tru immediately jumped in. "My words exactly."

It was late morning. Sasha sat primly on the sofa bed, now made up as a couch again, watching Waterman take a slurping swallow of steaming hot black coffee from a disposable cup. Two more cups and a couple of doughnuts sat untouched on the coffee table in front of Tru and Sasha, compliments of the FBI. Sasha was too wound up to eat, Tru too distraught.

Waterman eyed one of the doughnuts and Sasha smiled, gesturing for him to help himself. He plucked up the one with the honey glaze and took a big bite. He'd almost finished chewing when he raised his eyebrows. "Like I said, it's crazy, but it might work."

"And then again, it *might not* work," Tru retorted. "And Sasha would very likely end up getting caught in the cross fire."

Waterman finished off the doughnut and looked across at Sasha. "How are you going to lure them there?"

"They are all looking for me," Sasha explained calmly. "I will let one of them find me. And the others, I am sure, will follow."

"No," Tru said, springing up from the couch. "They'll find me."

"Tru."

"Must you always argue with me, Sasha?"

"I must do this. I am the one who is responsible—"

"You're no match for those creeps—"

"And you are?"

Waterman coughed, having swallowed down his coffee too fast. "Please, please. I get enough of this at home. Three teenagers. It's enough to drive a sane man crazy. Let's all just sit down nice and calm and talk this over like reasonable adults."

They tried their best, but within a minute Sasha and Tru were at it again, and Waterman was losing ground fast. But their arguing was cut off by a firm knock on their front door. The agent's hand went automatically to his gun until he heard a familiar voice identifying himself.

"Chief, it's me. Milton. Got something."

Waterman unlocked and opened the door. Milton, sweaty and a little out of breath from climbing three flights, handed a slip of paper over to his superior.

"It was in their mailbox back at the hotel. The desk clerk said a kid delivered it about an hour ago."

Sasha and Tru watched nervously as Waterman read the note. It couldn't have contained more than a few lines, yet he seemed to take forever to finish it.

"What is it?" Tru asked as Waterman finally turned around to face them.

"You have a grandmother?"

Tru suddenly went cold. The color drained from his face. Sasha reached for his hand. It was clammy.

"Tru's grandmother's name is—"

Before Sasha could finish, Waterman cut in. "Jessica Fortune?"

Tru broke free of Sasha's grasp and grabbed for the note.

"It's okay, Chief. It's been dusted for prints," Milton said.

Tru was already reading the few lines of typing on the sheet. "We'll call it an even exchange. Jessica Fortune for the icon. Grandma knows we mean business. We'll be in touch." There was no signature.

Tru's hand dropped limply to his side. Sasha retrieved the note. There was a pained expression on her face as she finished reading it.

"Oh, no. How could this be true?" Her voice was strained.

Tru strode over to the telephone and dialed his grandmother's Denver number. He took in a steadying breath as the phone rang. "It's Tru. Is my grandmother in?"

That was all he said. A few minutes later he hung up. "She left for Seattle this morning." His voice was a strained whisper. "She thought she'd come see how we were doing." His hands were trembling. He laced his fingers together. "I should have called her again. But I didn't want her to worry. I didn't want her to know we were in any danger. And I didn't want to...lie to her. But I should have called again. Maybe if I'd called..."

Sasha clutched his hands in hers, her voice overwrought. "You are not to blame. It is me. All of this is my fault. First I put you in jeopardy. Now your grandmother. If you had not come with me..." Her eyes filled with tears.

Seeing her pained expression, Tru pulled her to him. "Let's not stand here blaming ourselves, darling. We've got a plan, don't we? It'll work. She'll be okay. We'll all be okay." His voice was soft, gentle, assuring. Then he kissed her, mindless of the presence of the two federal agents. Sasha's sweet warm breath mingled with his, giving him much-needed strength and confidence in his own words.

Sasha felt it, too. She drew back and smiled up at Tru. "We shall proceed as planned, yes? Only now we do not have to worry about them finding us."

Waterman cleared his throat. "Right. Looks like we'll be cutting right to the chase." He looked over at Milton, who was busy inspecting the scuff marks on his cordovans. "Pack 'em up and move them back to the hotel. And tell the boys to keep a low profile over there," Waterman barked. "It's a good plan. And we'll all do our parts."

"I THINK THE WAITING is the worst part of all of this," Tru said, pacing up and down their hotel sitting room.

Sasha wasn't pacing, but she felt equally on edge as she sat on the sofa. She stared over at the phone on the table beside her as if she could somehow will it to ring.

Tru checked his watch. It was nearly three in the afternoon. The note had arrived at nine-fifteen that morning. What was taking them so long? *Them?* He wasn't even sure who would call. Lawrence? Bartov? Deidre? Which of them had kidnapped his grandmother? And which of them would be more likely to do her any harm?

He shook that awful possibility from his mind. It was a simple swap. His grandmother for the icon. The only hitch was—there was no icon. Waterman had told him not to worry about that little point. Sasha would draw a picture of the icon from memory and they'd have a fake one ready for the countdown. And as Waterman had so confidently said, "Before they even know they've been duped, they'll be in handcuffs."

With each passing moment of silence, Sasha was losing her confidence. She kept worrying about Jessica. The woman seemed in good health, but would the strain of what she was going through make her ill? Or worse? Oh, if only the phone would ring.

When it did ring, about twenty minutes later, they both jumped. Sasha, who was closer, went to reach for it, while Tru hurried into the bedroom to listen on the extension. Somewhere in another part of the hotel, Milton and Fleming were also at a hookup, monitoring the call. Sasha knew she must try to keep the caller on the line long enough for the agents to trace its source.

Her hand was trembling as she lifted the receiver to her ear, but her voice was clear and unwavering.

"Yes?"

"Do we have a deal?" came a raspy voice from the other end of the line. The words seemed deliberately muffled so that it was impossible even for Sasha to detect whether the caller had a Russian accent.

"I insist upon first speaking to Mrs. Fortune," Sasha replied.

Silence. Sasha's heart pounded against her chest. She could only imagine the tension Tru was experiencing.

And then . . .

"Hello? Tru? Sasha?"

"Jessica . . . ?"

"Granny . . . ?"

Jessica Fortune's expelled breath whistled through the wire. "Thank heaven you two are all right."

Tru gripped the receiver tightly. "Thank heaven we're all right? It's you we're worried about, Granny. We're sick with worry."

"There's no need to worry, dear. I'm fine. It's just . . ."

Another silence. This one lasted only a moment.

"So, are we on?" Once again, it was the muffled, raspy voice.

"Yes," Sasha said. "Tonight. I have the icon hidden at Fortune's Department Store on Westlake Avenue. The store closes at six. We will leave open the delivery door, which is on Pine Street. This leads into the men's clothing department. We will make the exchange there."

Again a silence. But Sasha could hear breathing.

When the muffled words came, they were strident. "You better be alone. No boyfriend, no cops. No funny business. Got it? Or Grandma gets it."

"Yes, just me," Sasha answered. "No funny business."

The phone clicked dead—and too soon to complete a trace.

12

TRU STUDIED HIMSELF closely in the mirror. Then he reached for some more hair gel. A little dab wasn't enough to keep his dark, unruly hair slicked back and shiny. He applied some more, picked up his already greasy comb and ran it through his hair, making sure to obliterate any hint of a part. *Better*, he thought. *Now for a couple of finishing touches.*

The bathroom doorknob jiggled. "Be out in a minute, Sasha."

"Are you okay, Tru?" she asked anxiously from behind the locked door.

"Fine. Just fine."

Sasha frowned. After the phone call from the smuggler cum kidnapper, she and Tru had gotten into a terrible row over his participation in tonight's "caper." Sasha had insisted it was too risky for him to be present. Tru had insisted it was too risky for him not to be there. Unfortunately, Waterman had agreed with Sasha. The agent tried to assure him that the operation would go like clockwork unless Tru was spotted, thus tipping the bad guys off.

"We'll have our boys all over the men's department," Waterman had told him. "And a bunch more surrounding the building to pick up any stray smugglers that come along. You want things to go smoothly, don't you? You don't want any slipups. It's going to be a pretty tense situation, as it is. But, I don't want you to worry now. We're going to pull it off."

Sasha had watched Tru's expression the whole time the agent was trying to convince him to stay put and let the professionals handle things. But she couldn't get a reading. Then, as soon as Waterman had left the hotel room, so had Tru. "A few things I need," he'd muttered obliquely, coming back about a half-hour later with a few small purchases. Sasha had tried to take a peek into the bags, but Tru had whisked them away and into the bathroom with him.

She knocked lightly on the bathroom door. "Tru. You are not thinking about any . . . funny business now." Her voice was colored with suspicion and concern.

There was no response, but she could hear him moving about behind the door. "I must leave soon, Tru."

Then the door opened. Sasha drew back with a start as a sinister-looking man with a pencil-thin mustache and slicked-back hair exited the bathroom. He wore a black shirt, black trousers, white tie. And a diabolical smile.

Of course, she recognized him a moment later. But for that one instant . . .

"Not bad, huh?" Tru asked, smiling a mobster smile, then plucking a stogie out of his pocket and sticking one end into the corner of his mouth.

"You promised, Tru."

"No, I didn't. I never make promises I don't intend to keep."

"Please, Tru . . ."

"Did I ever tell you the one about the mobster who was brought into the precinct for questioning?"

She sighed with frustration. "This is not a time for jokes, Tru. You must listen to reason. We must—"

"So, the next morning, the chief calls his two boys into his office and he says, 'So, what happened? What'd ya learn?' And the two cops shuffled their feet and shrugged—"

"I do not want to hear this joke, Tru. I want you to wash your hair and remove that ridiculous mustache. You cannot do this, Tru. It is too . . . risky. Bartov, Lawrence, Deidre Baker . . . Any one of them could show up and they would all recognize you. . . ."

"'Gee, Chief,' the cops said, 'we browbeat and badgered the bozo for hours. . . .' 'So, what did ya get?' the chief demanded. And one of the cops shrugs and says, 'Well he dozed off and kept muttering, "Yes, dear. I know, dear. Whatever you say, dear . . ."'" Tru grinned.

Sasha merely raised a brow. "That is the punch line?"

"You don't get it?"

"I do not find this joke amusing."

He moved toward her. "Okay, I'll try again. There's the joke about the two gunmen. . . ."

"No more bad jokes, Tru."

"Okay, no more bad jokes," he said, his tone and expression dead serious. "Listen to me, Sasha. The two women I love most in the world are in jeopardy. My grandmother and . . . you. There's no way I'm going to sit here twiddling my thumbs while the two of you are off at Fortune's putting your lives on the line. And that's the last word we're having on this topic, yes?" He softened his tone a little, even managing a small smile as he imitated her phrasing.

"No," she said firmly.

"Sasha, give it a rest."

"There is one more word on this topic," she told him. "I love you, too."

He leaned closer, half whispering, "Yes." And then he pulled her into his arms, dipping her in a sexy dance maneuver as he kissed her.

She was a little shaky as he brought her upright again. "I've got to go now," he said, smoothing back her hair, then running his index finger lightly over her just-kissed lips. "I'll see you there."

He was gone before she could protest. But there was no protest left in her, anyway. A few minutes later the phone rang. It was Waterman.

"We've got the icon stashed in the jacket pocket of the mannequin closest to register two. It's a blond dummy wearing . . ."

"I will be able to tell which is the dummy," Sasha said, cutting him off.

Waterman cleared his throat. "Let's hope no one else can."

BETWEEN FOUR AND SIX o'clock, a dozen federal agents ambled intermittently through the doors of the Fortune's Department Store on Westlake Avenue. They mingled with hundreds of other shoppers on all six floors. One of the first to arrive was Ron Waterman. After milling about the men's department for twenty minutes, he made his way up to the executive offices on the seventh floor, heading directly for the office of executive assistant, Dennis Drake.

Tru slipped into the store at about the same time Waterman was upstairs showing Drake his ID. By the time Tru got to Drake's door, he could hear the supercilious middle-aged exec sputtering, "Remove all the mannequins? And you want to do what?"

Tru opened the door. At first neither Drake nor Waterman recognized him. But once it struck the agent that the intruder looked a little like Al Capone, he quickly put two and two together. "Oh, no. No way. You've got twelve mannequins down in the men's department and I've got twelve agents, myself included, at the ready."

"Look, what's going on here?" Dennis Drake demanded.

He was all but ignored as Tru and Waterman eyed each other defiantly.

"You can send one of your boys home," Tru said firmly. "I'll be as good a dummy as any of your boys," he added with a gangster twang.

"Look here, Fortune . . ." Waterman started.

"Fortune?" gasped the distraught executive assistant. And then he looked more closely at the man with the greased-back hair and the dark mustache. "Why, it is you, Mr. Fortune. But . . . I don't understand."

Tru turned to Drake and gave him a broad smile. "It's all very simple, Den. I'm having what you could call a little surprise party tonight. Here at the store. In the men's department. After hours."

Dennis Drake squinted at him. "Didn't I read a while back about one of your brothers doing that? Throwing a big after-hours party in your Denver store?"

"Adam. Yes, he did throw quite a bash, but I'm talking about something much more . . . low-key."

"Twelve FBI agents are coming and you call it low-key?" Dennis demanded with amazement.

Tru merely smiled.

The executive assistant dabbed at his damp forehead with a linen hankie. "I still don't understand why the mannequins have to be removed. . . ."

Tru winked at him. "Why, Den, that's where the surprise comes in."

SASHA STILL HAD A half hour to go before she was to leave for Fortune's. As she waited, she made resolutions. As soon as this awful business was settled tonight, she would leave for Moscow. It would be unbearable saying good-bye to Tru, but it would be even more difficult later.

She rose abruptly from the small settee. But, what if she didn't leave? She loved Tru. And he loved her.

She sank back onto the settee. Yes, he loved her. But that didn't mean he would literally give up his fortune for her. And she had no right to ask that of him; she had no claim on him. Besides, hadn't she vowed never to make such a foolish mistake as to marry again? Especially an American.

But this time was different. She knew it and Tru knew it. Sasha remembered how her grandmother Leila had always believed that for each person there was one great love of their life. For Leila, it had been Sasha's grand-father, Yuri. And Sasha knew without a doubt that for her it was Tru. But unlike Leila, for her there would be no happy ending. She would return to her daily routine in Moscow, and she would live alone. Tru had spoiled her for anyone else. She rubbed her arms—it was the chill of the air conditioner and nerves. And longing.

She closed her eyes, trying to force back the desire ig-nited by just the thought of him. She mustn't let her feel-ings overwhelm her. She needed to be clearheaded and unemotional to face what lay ahead tonight. Soon, she would leave the hotel, take a taxi to Fortune's—

A knock on her door startled her.

"Who is there?"

"Fleming. Agent Fleming."

Sasha picked up a strained note in his voice and felt a rush of panic. Had something gone wrong?

She flung the door open only to discover that the agent was not alone. Standing beside Fleming, a gun pointed at the agent's temple, was the Russian, Bartov.

Fleming wore a pained expression as Bartov ushered him into the suite and shut the door. "He caught me off guard," the agent muttered.

Sasha smiled, but there was no humor in it. "Yes, he has that ability."

Bartov offered an equally humorless smile. "So we meet again, comrade. I hope this will be our final meeting."

Sasha instinctively stepped back, trying to suppress her panic. If Bartov was here, it had to be Lawrence, probably acting for Deidre Baker, who would be showing up at Fortune's. And if Sasha didn't show up as expected, something terrible might happen. She felt physically ill about the danger for Jessica and Tru if she didn't get away from Bartov and arrive at the store on schedule.

"Do not look so upset, dear comrade. I want only what was meant to be mine. Had Martin Baker lived, I am sure I could have convinced him to turn the icon over to my group. He was running scared from the first moment he spotted me in Moscow. I suspect his partners realized he was unreliable and took care of him. If you are not careful, they will take care of you, too."

"And you won't?" she answered defiantly, even though her whole body was trembling.

"You have the word of a fellow comrade that you will come to no harm on my account. For me this is strictly business—a very profitable business. Contraband items such as the one you possess are greatly sought after by certain foreign investors. I do not like to disappoint my customers, comrade. I merely want the icon and then I shall return to the motherland. I have anxious partners there waiting for the good word. Surely it is not your concern which group claims the piece. And think of it this way, comrade. At least you would remain loyal to your own people."

Sasha had all she could do not to spit on this poor excuse for a Russian citizen. With great effort she kept herself under control.

"You are right, comrade. I do not care. I want only to go home and put this terrible business behind me," Sasha said, injecting what she hoped was just the right note of weariness into her voice. "I will give you the icon, Bartov."

The Russian's eyes drifted to the bedroom door, a knowing smile playing across his face. "So, your playmate is in there."

Sasha wore a pleading expression. "No. He is not here. He left . . . nearly an hour ago." She gave Fleming a surreptitious glance. His expression was blank. She had no idea if he would be of any help to her or not.

Bartov grinned. "You are a very poor liar, comrade." He pushed Fleming aside, keeping his gun on him as he started for the bedroom door. Sasha, donning a truly frightened look now, hurried to block his passage.

"No," she cried, as he easily shoved her aside and grabbed for the doorknob. In his enthusiasm to walk in on Tru, Bartov forgot for a moment about Fleming and Sasha.

This was the moment Sasha had angled for and it couldn't be wasted, for there might not be another. Catching Bartov unawares, she stepped swiftly behind him, grabbed for his hair, snatching whole handfuls, and to his utter surprise, yanked with all her might.

Bartov let out a cry of shock and pain as he teetered backward before losing his balance completely and crashing to the floor on his back. Before he could make a move, Sasha dropped to her knees square on his chest and reached for the gun that was still in his hand.

As she struggled with Bartov, Fleming, who'd been nearly as stunned as the Russian by her kung-fu maneuver, came back to life and dove into the melee. A few moments later, he came up with the gun and the Russian in tow.

Fleming gave her a look of deep admiration. Sasha merely nodded, then checked her watch. "I must go now. You will be all right, yes?" she asked Fleming.

He nodded sheepishly. "Thanks."

She smiled and opened the bedroom door, dashing in to get her purse. Bartov looked into the empty room, realized he'd been duped—by an amateur no less—and glared at Sasha as she dashed back out.

IT WAS SIX FIFTY-FIVE. Twelve agents were in position, each attired in the twenties-style mobster costume of his mannequin predecessor. Unlike their predecessors, however, they all had nineties-style weapons hidden on them. From his podium right near men's shirts, Tru could make out six of the agents in the store's dim night lighting. The other five were out of sight, but he could feel their presence and it gave him some measure of reassurance.

It was close to countdown. He gave the man he could spot a last check. Thanks to some expert assistance from a couple of Fortune's window dressers, all of the men had been made up and posed to look incredibly like real mannequins.

Sasha was standing across the aisle from Tru near register two, double-checking the placement of the phony icon. She had arrived at Fortune's ten minutes late. It was the worst ten minutes of Tru's life. And then when she'd told him and the others about Bartov, Tru cursed himself for not being able to be in two places at the same time. Still, she'd handled Bartov very adeptly without him, albeit with some last-minute help from Fleming. Sasha was truly a remarkable woman.

A wave of sorrow flooded him. This really was countdown. Soon, she would be gone. He could already feel the loss.

A faint creaking sound pulled him from his depressing thoughts. He gave Sasha one last glance. This time she met his gaze and smiled confidently. Yes, she truly was remarkable.

Sasha was thinking much the same about Tru as she saw six men enter the men's department. All of them, she was distressed to observe, had guns in their hands. But what was far more distressing was that Jessica Fortune was not with them.

One man broke from the pack and came toward her, his gun aimed directly at her. Even though she knew Tru was right there, as were eleven trained federal agents, Sasha had to swallow her terror, knowing that now, more than ever, she must stay clearheaded and not let fear overtake her.

"I really hope you've played it smart, sweetheart."

It was Jack Lawrence. His tone was flip, but the expression on his face was menacing.

"Where is she?" Sasha could hear the quaver in her voice.

"First, the boys need to make sure there's no funny business." He stepped in closer to her. Sasha cringed inwardly. He reached out for her. She shrank from his touch, but he held her in a strong grip, and his gun was pointed right at her temple. "Just in case you didn't play it smart."

Sasha forced herself not to look in Tru's direction, desperate not to give anything away. But she knew how he must be feeling; what he, too, was going through.

"I am alone, as we agreed. I think it would be best to conclude this transaction quickly and . . ."

Lawrence turned around to his accomplices. "Give the area a thorough check. Make sure we're alone." He turned back to Sasha as his men scattered. "Where's the boyfriend?"

Sasha bit unconsciously at her lower lip, praying that Lawrence's scouts wouldn't notice that the mannequins were so incredibly lifelike that . . .

"Hey, I asked you a question," Lawrence said impatiently.

Sasha felt the cold nudge of metal against her temple. "He is still at the hotel. He is waiting for my call. If I do not telephone him by seven-fifteen, he will know that something has gone wrong. He will then contact the authorities. Within minutes after his call, this store will be surrounded." Her voice was steadier now.

He snickered. "Think you're pretty smart, don't you?"

"And you think you are pretty smart, yes?"

"What's that supposed to mean?"

"You are working for Deidre Baker." Sasha, noting his loss of composure, went on. "I believe you are in love with her, yes? I believe, also, you murdered Bill Hovy for her."

A woman's voice came out from the shadows. "You're smarter than you look."

Sasha recognized the voice. It belonged to Deidre Baker. A moment later, the woman herself stepped out of the shadows.

"You are the ringleader, yes?"

"Yes," Deidre said offhandedly. "It started out being Martin, Bill Hovy and I. And a few trusted aides." She smiled provocatively at Lawrence, then turned back to Sasha.

"Unfortunately, Martin started getting cold feet," she went on blithely. "Especially after his last jaunt to Moscow. What with the phony marriage and that damn Bartov, the poor fellow came home quite undone. The boys, here, and I agreed that Martin was becoming a liability. We had to take care of that." Again she smiled at Lawrence—an approving smile this time.

"But you led Bill Hovy to believe it was Bartov who 'took care of' your husband, yes?" Sasha observed.

Deidre sneered. "I didn't have to lead Bill to that conclusion. Bill had a mordant fear of Russians. He knew Bartov was breathing down Martin's neck and he just assumed it was Bartov who killed him. Which made poor Bill panic. I knew Bill was going to try to persuade you to turn the icon over to Bartov in order to save his neck." She stroked Lawrence's shoulder. "Poor Bill. He really was between a rock and a hard place."

Lawrence grinned.

Sasha gave Lawrence a pitying look. "All this, and you are fool enough to believe you, too, are not expendable? Do you not see what plan she has in mind for you? A plan I believe she has always had in mind—"

"Shut up," Deidre snapped as Lawrence gave her an edgy look.

All it took was a sensual stroke from Deidre to calm his fears. Besides, he had the gun. "Hey," he called out to his men. "What's the word?"

To Sasha's great relief, one by one, Lawrence's henchmen gave an all-clear call. Lawrence called out one more order. "Okay. Phillips, Barkley, you know what to do."

Sasha's muscles tightened. What did Lawrence mean? *You know what to do.*

Lawrence smiled excitedly at Deidre. "Okay, babe. Let's make our swap and get out of here."

Deidre eyed Sasha without saying a word. Sasha held her breath. "Where's the icon?" she finally demanded.

"I can produce it. But first I must see Mrs. Fortune."

At last, Deidre nodded.

"Okay, bring the old bag in," Lawrence called out.

"Is that how you would like someone to address your grandmother?" Sasha accused with derision.

He laughed harshly. "She's been called worse."

Jessica Fortune looked remarkably calm as she entered the men's department and smiled reassuringly at Sasha. Sasha tried to smile back, but the smile dropped from her face as she saw Jessica's eyes come to rest on one of the mannequins. Of course, it was Tru. Sasha swallowed hard. This could be the end of her brilliant plan. The end of everything.

But then Jessica turned away from her grandson, a blank look on her face. Sasha couldn't be sure if she was a consummate actress or if she actually hadn't recognized Tru. At the moment, it didn't matter.

"Okay. The icon," Lawrence ordered.

Sasha looked over at Jessica, "Are you all right?"

Jessica smiled. "I am now, my dear."

Sasha focused on Deidre. "How do I know that you will not harm us once you have the icon?"

Deidre shrugged. "You don't. I guess you'll just have to trust me."

"Like your husband trusted you? Like Bill Hovy trusted you? Like Lawrence here trusts you?"

Lawrence gave her a glowering look. "Shut up."

Sasha merely shook her head. Then she extended her right hand, revealing the icon, reaching for Jessica at the same time with her left hand.

Sasha clasped Jessica's hand tightly as Lawrence snatched the icon from her.

"Give it to me," Deidre demanded.

Lawrence gave her a cool smile. "What's the hurry?"

"You know what the hurry's about, baby. It's getting hot around here," Deidre cooed.

That was when Sasha smelled the smoke. So that was what Lawrence's order to two of his men was about. He'd told them to start a fire in the store—a fire that she and Tru and Jessica were meant to die in. She felt Jessica's grip tighten on her hand. Jessica smelled the smoke, too.

"We got all the time in the world," Lawrence was saying to Deidre.

Deidre smiled sweetly at her partner in crime, plucking the icon from his hand. "I'm afraid the time is running out real fast for one of us, baby."

Everything happened in fast forward from the moment it finally dawned on Lawrence that he'd been duped by Deidre, just like Martin Baker and Bill Hovy before him. He swung his gun in Deidre's direction. But before he could fire a shot, three of his henchmen grabbed him. After all, it was Deidre who was footing the bill.

That was Sasha's chance to get herself and Jessica out of the fray. Tugging at the older woman's hand, she pulled her back a few yards and around the side of a large wooden bin displaying the new fall sweaters.

"Quick, get down." Even before Sasha finished, Jessica had dropped to the floor, taking Sasha with her and giving her a sprightly wink.

In the next instant, the pasty-faced "mannequins" came to life, taking Deidre, Lawrence and the half-dozen henchmen completely by surprise. Without a single shot, they were all summarily rounded up by a group of the best dressed federal agents in town, several of whom then raced off to extinguish the fire.

Tru found Sasha and his grandmother huddled behind the bin. He threw his arms around them both just as the sprinkler system released streams of water over them. They all laughed with relief.

Fortune's fire-damage insurance company was bound to take a more solemn view of the outcome.

"WHERE IS SHE?" Tru asked as soon as he stepped out of Waterman's office back at Seattle headquarters later that night. He, Sasha, and his grandmother had been there for hours giving lengthy statements.

"She left," Jessica said quietly, looking closely at her grandson.

"Left? You mean left for the hotel?"

Jessica rose, placing her hand on his arm. "She left for the airport, Tru. She's catching a plane for New York in an hour. And from there she's booked a flight for Moscow."

"Without even . . . saying goodbye?"

"I don't think she could bear saying goodbye to you." Jessica hesitated. "I don't think she *wanted* to say goodbye." She gave him a meaningful look.

"It's impossible, Gran. It wouldn't work. To sacrifice . . . everything?"

"Is it everything, Tru?" She pressed her palm to his cheek. It was warm to her touch. She searched his face. Oh, how she recognized all of the signs. "Or has 'everything,' just walked out of your life?"

He gave her a faint smile. "So this is what it was like for Adam and Pete," he mused. "I didn't get it. I couldn't begin to get it."

"Until now, you mean?"

He gave her a quick kiss. "I've got to hurry."

Jessica smiled as she watched him race off. Then she went to the pay phone in the hall to call her friend, Ben Engel in Chicago. She had a sudden longing to hear his voice. *So this is what it's like*, she mused as she dialed Ben's number.

TRU MADE ONE QUICK STOP at an all-night mall before racing to the airport. When he got to the gate for Flight 425 to New York, he saw that the passengers were already boarding through a long, narrow corridor. He tried to spot Sasha, but he couldn't see her in the crowd.

The young woman attendant at the boarding-pass counter gave him a wary look as he hurriedly approached. "My girlfriend's getting on the plane. I've got to talk to her. It's an emergency. Life or death." He meant it, too.

The young woman stepped back, looked around nervously. Only then did Tru realize that his face was still streaked with the pasty makeup that had given him the required lifeless look of a mannequin. He tried for a bright smile to compensate for his ghoulish complexion.

"I was in a play tonight. Please...just let me go through and see if I can spot her. I just need to give her a message."

But the woman wasn't looking at him. She was nodding to a security guard who was about thirty feet away. Tru knew he had to do something fast. And he did.

He whipped out his newly purchased boom-box recorder from a shopping bag, slipped in a tape, and turned up the volume knob as high as it would go.

It was "The Blue Danube" waltz by Strauss.

SASHA WAS HALFWAY down the boarding corridor when she heard the music. At first she thought it was being pumped in through speakers, courtesy of the airline. But then she stopped abruptly, nearly causing several passengers to collide with her.

"Excuse me. I am sorry. The music." She looked a bit dazed. "It is a . . . waltz, yes?" she asked the gray-haired woman who was trying to get by her.

"Waltz music? Isn't that nice? So much more pleasant than that awful rock and roll. . . ."

"Yes. Yes, it is nice. It is wonderful." Sasha hesitated, and passengers circled around her as she searched for the speakers in the corridor. But there were none. She looked back toward the gate area, but there were too many people blocking her view.

No, she thought. *It isn't possible.* But slowly, her heart racing, she began to thread her way through the crowd, retracing her steps.

She spotted Tru just as the security guard was about to drag him and his blasting tape player away. As soon as Tru saw her, he broke free. He and Sasha ran the distance separating them and fell into each other's arms.

"Oh, Tru. I could not say goodbye. . . ."

"You can't say goodbye, Sasha. I've still got so many jokes to tell you. . . ."

"You tell such terrible jokes, comrade," she murmured through her tears of joy.

"I know. I don't waltz much better. But—" he cupped her chin and looked at her for a long moment "—I'll improve with practice. If you'll be my dance partner, Sasha Malzeva. If you'll be my dance partner for life."

She looked up into his face and she saw only love there. "We have such different upbringing, different views, different ideas. We will argue a lot."

"We'll make up a lot."

"Oh, Tru. You will give up everything...?"

He pressed his lips to hers. "*You* are everything."

"Yes. For me, too," she murmured. "Nothing else matters to me so much as you. Not my work, my friends, not even my country."

He held her at arm's length. "Look, my grandfather came here from the Old Country without a dime and started up a business that became a multimillion-dollar enterprise. Why can't we do the same? We'll even go a step further. We'll make ours international. We'll bridge the gap between East and West." He drew her into his arms, holding her tight, knowing now that he would never let her go. "What do you say, Sasha?"

She looked up into his eyes. "I say, waltz with me, my darling comrade."

The security guard and the airline attendant who had heard most of the lovers' conversation smiled at each other as Sasha and Tru waltzed together in the middle of the terminal to the romantic strains of "The Blue Danube."

The Fortune Boys concludes in December, 1992 with Taylor Made, Temptation #424. *Reclusive Taylor Fortune's passion was his invention, Homer the robot. When PR exec Ali Spencer took on the marketing campaign, Taylor realized that there was a lot more to reproduction than nuts and bolts!*

HARLEQUIN®

Temptation®

Rebels & Rogues

Jared: He'd had the courage to fight in Vietnam. But did he have the courage to fight for the woman he loved?

THE SOLDIER OF FORTUNE
By Kelly Street
Temptation #421, December

All men are not created equal. Some are rough around the edges. Tough-minded but tenderhearted. Incredibly sexy. The tempting fulfillment of every woman's fantasy.

When it's time to fight for what they believe in, to win that special woman, our Rebels and Rogues are heroes at heart. Twelve Rebels and Rogues, one each month in 1992, only from Harlequin Temptation.

HARLEQUIN®
Temptation®

the Fortune Boys

A funny, sexy miniseries from bestselling
author Elise Title!

LOSING THEIR HEARTS MEANT
LOSING THEIR FORTUNES....

If any of the four Fortune brothers were unfortunate enough to
wed, they'd be permanently divorced from the Fortune
millions—thanks to their father's last will and testament.

BUT CUPID HAD OTHER PLANS!
Meet Adam in #412 **ADAM & EVE** (Sept. 1992)
Meet Peter #416 **FOR THE LOVE OF PETE**
(Oct. 1992)
Meet Truman in #420 **TRUE LOVE** (Nov. 1992)
Meet Taylor in #424 **TAYLOR MADE** (Dec. 1992)

WATCH THESE FOUR MEN TRY TO WIN
AT LOVE AND NOT FORFEIT $$$

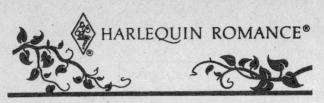

HARLEQUIN ROMANCE®

After her father's heart attack, Stephanie Bloomfield comes home to Orchard Valley, Oregon, to be with him and with her sisters.

Orchard Valley

Steffie learns that many things have changed in her absence—but not her feelings for journalist Charles Tomaselli. He was the reason she left Orchard Valley. Now, three years later, will he give her a reason to stay?

"The Orchard Valley trilogy features three delightful, spirited sisters and a trio of equally fascinating men. The stories are rich with the romance, warmth of heart and humor readers expect, and invariably receive, from Debbie Macomber."

—Linda Lael Miller

Don't miss the Orchard Valley trilogy by Debbie Macomber:

VALERIE Harlequin Romance #3232 (November 1992)
STEPHANIE Harlequin Romance #3239 (December 1992)
NORAH Harlequin Romance #3244 (January 1993)

Look for the special cover flash on each book!

Available wherever Harlequin books are sold. ORC-2